JUNIOR
HIGH

THOSE
CRAZY
CLASS
PICTURES

JUNIOR HIGH

Junior High Jitters
Class Crush
The Day the Eighth Grade Ran the School
How Dumb Can You Get?
The Eighth Grade to the Rescue
Eighth Grade Hero?
Those Crazy Class Pictures

#7

JUNIOR HIGH

THOSE CRAZY CLASS PICTURES

Kate Kenyon

SCHOLASTIC INC.
New York Toronto London Auckland Sydney

ISBN 0-590-41160-8

12 11 10 9 8 7 6 5 4 3 2 1   7 8 9/8 0 1 2/9

Printed in the U.S.A.   01

First Scholastic printing, November 1987

Chapter 1

Jennifer Mann tucked a lock of her long dark hair behind her ear. "What's Lucy doing inside?" she wondered aloud.

"Inside *school*?" her best friend, Nora Ryan, asked incredulously.

Unless it was a dire emergency, none of the eighth-graders passed through the Cedar Groves Junior High double front doors until the bell rang. Yet, just inside the door, Lucy Armanson was gesturing wildly.

Nora stood on tiptoe to see over the heads of her taller classmates. "She's looking right at us," she said. "Do you suppose she's trying to tell us something?"

"Like what?"

"I don't know. Maybe she's got a new outfit she wants to show us."

Lucy kept up with all the latest trends and always looked as though she'd stepped out of the pages of *Seventeen*.

"I don't think so," Jennifer said. Although it was hard to tell for sure through the grimy glass doors, it looked as though Lucy was wearing her Guess jeans and her striped rugby shirt.

Amy Williams came up beside them. "Lucy doing her aerobics early?" she asked as she jogged in place. Amy wanted to be a gym teacher, and she was always in practice.

Nora shrugged. "We were just trying to figure it out. I think she's trying to tell us something."

"Why doesn't she just come out here and tell us?" Jennifer said.

"Beats me," Nora said. She smiled at Lucy and waved.

Lucy rolled her eyes and pulled back her lips in a desperate grimace. It was hopeless. She'd been trying to get Jennifer and Nora's attention for minutes, and they just stood there, gaping at her.

Tommy Ryder poked his head around the door. "Hey, Lucy, you don't have to go through all those moves to get my attention," he said. "If you wanna talk to me, just say so."

Lucy groaned. Tommy Ryder was the most conceited boy in the eighth grade. "I'll do that," she said. "And until I do, get lost." She picked up her bookbag from the floor and held it up threateningly.

Tommy backed off, letting the door slam behind him.

Alternately pointing at the girls and beckoning to them, Lucy mouthed, "Jennifer! Nora!"

"Now what's she doing?" Amy said.

"Maybe she's got some nerve disease," Nora said. "One that interferes with normal muscle control." Nora hoped to be a doctor and was always interested in symptoms.

"Since yesterday?" Amy said.

"There are diseases like that," Nora assured her. "They sneak up on you. You wake up one morning and POW! you've got something. My grandmother's arthritis started that way."

Saying, "I'm going to find out what her problem is," Jennifer walked toward the doors.

Nora and Amy followed her.

Lucy opened the door a crack and leaned out. "Quick!" she urged. "Come inside!"

"But the bell hasn't — !" Jennifer's protest was cut off when Lucy grabbed her arm and pulled her into the hall.

Nora and Amy squeezed in after her.

"This better be good," Nora said.

Lucy led the way down the main corridor. "You won't believe it. I'm not sure I do, and I saw it with my own eyes."

"Saw what?" Jennifer asked.

"You'll see," Lucy said. "Unless I'm seeing things."

Nora halted abruptly, planting both feet firmly on the worn tile floor. "I'm not taking another step until you tell me what you're talking about," she said.

Behind her, Jennifer let out a surprised gasp. "Is that who I think it is?"

"I don't believe I'm seeing what I'm seeing," Amy said.

Lucy said, "Can you believe it? Right here in the front hall?"

Nora turned her head. There on the bulletin board reserved for important announcements was a big picture of Tracy Douglas. A *very* big picture of Tracy Douglas!

The girls stepped closer for a better look. Tracy was a pretty blonde with a wide-eyed, innocent look. This picture captured her least flattering expression.

"It's not very good," Jennifer said.

Nora, who did not share Jennifer's sense of loyalty to Tracy, said, "She looks as spacy as ever."

"It's the picture," Jennifer said in Tracy's defense. "It's so . . . fuzzy."

A voice behind them said, "Just like Tracy." It was Susan Hillard, who stood looking over Lucy's shoulder. Behind them were rows of eighth-graders, all craning their necks for a better look. And the crowd kept growing.

Andy Warwick and Mia Stevens, in matching rainbow-spiked hair and black vinyl pants, pushed to the front of the group.

"That is *some* kind of picture," Andy said.

Mia, who'd been his girl friend since seventh grade, elbowed him in the ribs.

"The question is, *what* kind?" Susan said.

"What's everybody doing in here?" Lucy demanded.

"Bell rang," Joan said.

"I didn't hear it." Lucy looked at Jennifer and Nora. "Did you hear it?"

The girls shook their heads.

"Too busy admiring the artwork," Susan said sarcastically.

Tommy Ryder and Mitch Pauley sauntered up.

Wearing his lopsided "Here I am — just what you've been waiting for, girls" smile, Tommy stepped in front of the group. "Sorry to keep you all waiting," he said.

Mitch Pauley's mouth dropped open when he saw Tracy's picture. "Hey, hey," he said. "What's this?"

"My fan club," Tommy responded.

The girls snickered.

Mitch stared at the bulletin board.

"That's my place," he said. Mitch had been voted the class's best all-around athlete. Until now, his picture had been on the bulletin board above the athletic events calendar.

Still unaware of the picture, Tommy said, "You have to find your own groupies, Mitch. These are mine."

"I'm talking about this picture," Mitch informed his friend.

Tommy turned. "Well, whaddya know? Tracy Douglas, my most ardent admirer. I'll bet she was looking at me when that picture was taken."

"Right," Susan said. "That explains the stupefied look on her face."

"Where *is* Tracy?" Jennifer asked.

"She had an appointment this morning," Amy replied.

"With who?" Nora asked. It had to be serious to take time off from school.

Amy shrugged. "She didn't say."

Mia leaned close to the bulletin board. "Did you see this?" She indicated an announcement beside Tracy's picture. "It's about the new camera club. I'll bet Tracy's picture has something to do with that."

Susan Hillard guffawed.

"It makes sense," Nora said. "This announcement's been up at least two weeks. Who's paid any attention? Look at the sign-up sheet; it's blank."

"Maybe Tracy's the model or something," Jennifer said.

Tommy Ryder liked that idea. "Gimme a pen," he said to no one in particular. "I've always wanted to be a photographer."

Some of the other boys formed a loose line behind him.

"Aren't you going to sign up?" Mia asked Andy. Her tone said, *You'd better not*.

"Nah," Andy said. "Clubs like that are for amateurs."

"I suppose you're a pro," Lucy said.

Andy shrugged, adjusted the dog collar he wore around his neck, and sauntered off.

"What do you think, Jen?" Nora asked. "Should we join?"

"I don't know," Jennifer said. It might be fun to learn something about photography, but it meant another meeting. She already had her projects — Save the Whales, visits to the old people's home, entertaining at the orphanage — and all of them required meetings. Could she possibly fit in another? "I'll think about it," she said.

Jason Anthony careened toward the group on his skateboard. "Heads up!" he warned. "I can't stop!" He had broken his ankle a few weeks before. Now, wearing a walking cast, his control was uncertain.

The crowd scattered. At full throttle, Jason sailed past. Someone shouted, "Creep!" Jason looked back to smirk at his classmates, whose expressions transformed from annoyance to horror as Mr. Donovan, the principal, emerged from his office. Jason plowed into him, knocking the breath from both of them.

"Oooofff!" the man said.

Thinking he said, "Off!" Jason said, "Yes, sir. Right away, sir," as he clumsily complied.

"Well, Mr. Anthony, I suppose you're going to tell me you were doing a physics experiment," Mr. Donovan said.

"Actually, sir, I wasn't going to tell you that," Jason said. Because I didn't think of it, he added silently.

Mr. Donovan glared at him, waiting for more. "Because. . . ." Jason sighed. ". . . because . . . I was keeping it for a surprise. It's a . . . special project. Extra credit. All about . . . irresistible forces and . . . immovable objects." He was safe with that; it sounded scientific and . . . familiar.

"A worthy investigation," Mr. Donovan said kindly.

Jason smiled. He was actually going to get away with this!

"And I think you'll find," Mr. Donovan continued, his lips becoming narrower and tighter with every word, "that when an irrestible force like you meets an immovable object like me. . . ."

Suddenly, Jason remembered why the line sounded familiar: It wasn't a scientific principle at all; he'd heard it on an old record of his mother's! He smiled sheepishly. " 'Something's gotta give,' " he finished.

Mr. Donovan nodded and held out his hand.

Reluctantly, Jason gave him his skateboard.

Everyone clapped. Finally, Jason had been caught. Skateboards were strictly forbidden inside school, but somehow, Jason had always managed to break the rule without consequence.

Mr. Donovan directed his attention to the audience. "I suggest the rest of you follow Jason's example and do a little physics experiment of your own. In velocity — which, you might remember, is the distance a moving object travels with respect to time."

People took off in all directions, heading for their homerooms.

"What did you think of Tracy's picture?" Nora asked Denise Hendrix at lunch.

"The one on the bulletin board in the

main hall?" Denise asked. "Didn't see it."

"Then how do you know where it is?" Lucy asked.

"Because that's all anybody's talking about."

Amy was incredulous. "And you haven't seen it? How could you miss it?"

"Tony dropped me off at the side door this morning." Tony was Denise's foxy sixteen-year-old brother. He was a sophomore at Cedar Groves High School, which was connected to the junior high by a long corridor.

"But you've had all morning!" Amy said.

"I haven't had a reason to go past that bulletin board," Denise explained.

"To see Tracy's picture," Lucy said. "That's been everybody's reason since I discovered it this morning."

Jennifer studied Denise's beautiful heart-shaped face and flawless skin. "You'd make a good model," she said to Denise. "You ought to join."

"Model for what?" Denise asked. "Join what?"

"The photography club," Jennifer explained. "We figured that's why Tracy's picture is on the board right next to the sign-up sheet."

"If I joined the photography club,"

Denise said, "it'd be to *take* pictures, not pose for them."

"I didn't know you were interested in photography," Lucy said.

"I'm not."

Lucy was confused. "But you just said — "

"I said *if* I was interested in photography, I'd want to *take* pictures, wouldn't I? I'd want to be a *photographer* not just a model!" Denise told her.

That really annoyed Susan. Sometimes Denise was a real pain. Her parents owned Denise Cosmetics, and she had lived all over the world; consequently, Denise was a year older than her classmates. She thinks she's better than everyone else, Susan thought. In her most patronizing tone, she said, "Touchy, touchy."

Denise sighed. She probably deserved that. "Can you blame me?" she said. "This place is crazy today. Everybody's so hyper — all talking about some picture or other — "

"Tracy's picture," Amy said. "We told you that."

"*Every*body's told me that!" Denise said. She bit into her egg salad sandwich.

"I don't know how you can eat that," Nora said.

Denise stopped chewing and examined

her sandwich, as though Nora knew something about it she didn't.

"I thought eggs were good for you," Jennifer said.

"Full of cholesterol. And with all that mayonnaise — "

Purposely changing the subject before Nora could launch into one of her nutrition lectures, Lucy said, "What I want to know is, where's Tracy?"

"She had some kind of appointment," Amy said.

"You don't believe that, do you?" Susan asked.

"Of course I believe it. Why wouldn't I believe it?"

"Because it's obviously a cover-up," Susan explained.

"For what?" Jennifer asked.

Suddenly the center of attention, Susan sat back. Looking from one to another, she said, "Tracy put that picture up herself, and she's not here because she can't face the consequences."

Shocked exclamations shot through the group.

"That's crazy," Nora said.

"Why would she do that?" Jennifer asked.

"For attention," Susan said.

"From what I hear," Denise put in, "it's not a very good picture."

"Right," Amy said. "If she did it herself, wouldn't she have picked a better picture?"

"Maybe that's what she *wanted* us to think," Susan explained.

"Tracy isn't like that," Jennifer said.

"You mean she isn't . . . smart enough?" Susan needled.

"Sly enough," Jennifer snapped.

"There she is now!" Lucy exclaimed.

All heads turned to see Tracy standing uncertainly just inside the cafeteria. Usually smiling, Tracy's mouth was tightly closed and her face was pinched.

Lucy got to her feet. "I'll find out what's going on."

"Wait!" Jennifer said. "There's something wrong."

"That's for sure," Amy said. "Steve Crowley's standing right next to her, and she doesn't even know it."

"She knows it all right," Susan said. "It's an act — part of her plan. Miss Boy-Crazy is going to play hard to get now, you just watch."

Lucy glared at her.

"She's not acting," Jennifer said. "Something's bothering her."

Lucy said, "Probably the picture."

As Tracy threaded her way toward them, Nora moved her chair to make room. "We'll soon find out," she said.

Chapter 2

Tommy Ryder slicked back his sandy brown hair when he saw Tracy at the cafeteria door. "Hey, Trace!" he called. "I'll have *my* camera tomorrow."

Tracy didn't hear him. Nor did she notice the other boys turning to look at her as she passed. Any other day, she would have been flattered by the attention; today, she was oblivious to it. Her whole attention was focused on making it to the group's table in the center of the cafeteria without anyone noticing her. It would be hard enough to face her good friends after the long, painful orthodontist appointment that morning, let alone the rest of the class.

"There sure is something wrong with Tracy," Amy said. "She didn't even hear Tommy."

"Just like I told you," Susan said smugly as Tracy approached. "An act."

Tracy slumped into a chair, put her elbows on the table, and her hands over her mouth. She mumbled something.

"What?" Amy asked.

Tracy repeated the words behind her hands.

"*We can't hear you, Tracy.*" Susan exaggerated each word.

Tracy lowered her hands. "I said, 'Hi, everybody.'" This time, she didn't move her lips.

"Are you practicing ventriloquism or what?" Lucy teased.

Tracy's blue eyes clouded. She was going to cry.

To ease the tension, Jennifer asked, "Did you have lunch?"

Tracy shook her head.

Nora pushed her prune whip toward the girl. "Have this. I'm full."

"Can't eat," Tracy said.

"I don't blame you," Lucy said. "That stuff is enough to make anyone lose her appetite."

The picture has upset her, Jennifer thought. "Tracy, it's not all that bad," she said sympathetically.

"Right," Nora said, referring to the dessert. "It's practically the only nutritious thing in this whole place."

"Nora," Jennifer said, amusement flashing in her hazel eyes, "I didn't mean the prune whip. It's . . . the other thing that's not so bad."

Nora nodded. "Oh," she said. "Jen's right, Tracy. Things could be worse."

Tracy dropped her head forward so that her shoulder-length blonde hair fell over her face. Her mouth hurt. "No, they couldn't. I'll probably never eat again." This was, without a doubt, the worst day of her life.

"Sure you will," Nora assured her. "No matter how depressed a person is, that person eventually eats something. The will to survive is very strong in the human species."

Tracy shook her head slowly.

The others exchanged hopeless glances. Tracy was usually so bubbly; today she was flat. She was obviously hurting. That, too, was unlike her. Although she was sensitive to criticism, she was quick to recover. And the picture on the bulletin board in the front hall couldn't even be considered a criticism.

Jennifer twisted a lock of her long hair around her index finger. Because she had always liked Tracy and often defended her against their classmates' teasing, Jennifer was particularly disturbed by this change in the girl. The picture, unflattering as it was, couldn't have affected her this way; it must be something else. "Are you sick?" she asked.

Tracy shook her head.

"You're just . . . not hungry — is that it?"

Tracy raised her head. "I'm starved," she said. "I just can't eat." She lowered her head again. "I'll never be able to eat. I can't even chew gum!"

Lucy frowned. What did chewing gum have to do with the picture on the bulletin board in the main hall? "Gum?" she said. "Gum!"

Susan smiled smugly. She had been right: Tracy must have tacked the picture on the bulletin board herself; why else would she be acting this way? "Then why'd you do it?"

"It wasn't my idea," Tracy said.

"Sure," Susan said, "I'll bet you mother made you do it."

Tracy's head snapped up. "You *know*!" she said, her eyes wide and her lips barely moving. Her mouth throbbed with pain.

"Everybody *knows*," Denise said. "That's all they're talking about."

"Who told them?" Tracy said.

"Listen," Susan said as she got to her feet, "nobody told anybody anything. We can all see, you know."

Tracy clamped both hands over her mouth.

"You didn't expect to get away with it, did you?" Susan continued. "If a person does a thing like that herself — "

"Myself?" Tracy interrupted, her hands laced protectively in front of her mouth. "I wouldn't do a thing like this *myself*! How could I? I don't even have the . . . tools."

"All it takes is a tack," Susan said.

"And maybe a stool," Amy added. "Unless Tracy can really stretch, she couldn't reach without one. And a camera, of course."

Susan stormed off, leaving Tracy totally confused. She looked helplessly from one friend to another.

Jennifer put her hand on Tracy's arm. "Susan thinks you put the picture up yourself."

"Picture?" Tracy asked. "What picture?"

There was a long pause while the girls tried to sort through the conversation. Finally, Nora said, "Tracy, let's start from the beginning. You came in here a few minutes ago looking as though you'd been through some . . . trauma — "

"You could tell?" Tracy was horrified. "Even at a distance?"

"We knew *something* was wrong. Steve

Crowley was standing right next to you —
looking at you," Amy recounted, "and you
didn't even — "

"Steve Crowley? Oh, no!" Tracy slid
down in her chair and glanced around the
cafeteria. Steven was one of the best-
looking boys in the whole class and nice,
too. She'd been trying to get his attention
all year. And today, on the one day she
wanted to be invisible, he had noticed her.
Life was unfair. "Do you think he knows?"
she said. "I'll die if Steve Crowley knows."

Denise sighed. Sometimes, being four-
teen in a class of thirteen-year-olds could
be trying. She summoned all the patience in
her to say, "Tracy, you're making too much
out of this."

"Steve's real understanding," Jennifer
assured her.

"Right," Nora agreed.

The two of them had been friends with
Steve since kindergarten. They had always
been comfortable with him. He was easy to
talk to as boys went, and they could always
count on him to be supportive. He certainly wouldn't tease Tracy about her
picture.

"He's much too mature to flip over some
picture," Jennifer said.

Tracy blinked. "Picture? What picture?" she said again.

Lucy sighed and ran her hand through

her curly black hair. "The one of you on the announcement bulletin board," she said.

"We figured it had something to do with the camera club," Nora said. "Sort of like advertising to draw attention to the sign-up sheet."

"It sure worked," Amy said. "Practically everybody signed up."

"We thought maybe you were going to be a model or something," Jennifer put in.

The words swirled so fast around her that Tracy couldn't catch hold. "My picture?" she said. "Model?"

"You mean you don't know anything about it?" Nora asked. Although she didn't mean it to, it sounded like an accusation.

Tracy's lower lip jutted into a pout. "I wasn't here this morning," she said slowly. "I had an — "

" — appointment," Amy said. "I told everybody that, but Susan thought — "

"It's not a bad picture," Jennifer interrupted to save Tracy from a rehash of Susan's speculation. Obviously, Tracy could not have tacked the picture up there herself; she didn't know a thing about it. Whatever was bothering her had nothing to do with the picture. "You're much prettier and it's really fuzzy, but it's kind of an honor, don't you think? I mean, except for

Mitch Pauley's picture — who else's has been up there?"

"Mine," Amy said.

"That was different," Lucy pointed out. "The girls' basketball team — a *group* picture."

Tracy's face relaxed. "My picture in the front hall," she said, trying the idea before deciding how she felt about it.

Everyone waited for her reaction. Not one of them was sure how *she'd* feel if someone had plastered her picture up for everyone to see.

Tracy stood up. "Let's go see it," she said. And, forgetting the morning's appointment and her earlier discomfort at coming to school at all today, she smiled.

Jennifer gasped. "Tracy, you have — "

" — braces!" the others exclaimed.

Chapter 3

"Braces!" Amy Williams said. "Why didn't you tell me your appointment was with the ortho?"

Tracy sat down, the smile frozen on her face, her shiny silver braces gleaming in the fluorescent light. "I didn't want anyone to know," she said, and clamped her hands over her mouth.

"Lots of people have braces," Denise said. "Probably half the class."

"My aunt has them and she's fifty!" Amy said.

Nora croaked. "Susan ... Tracy — " She choked on the words.

"Nora!" Jennifer said, beginning to laugh. "Stop it!"

Nora took a deep breath and began again. "Tracy was talking about the braces!"

"So?" Denise said.

"Susan was talking about the picture! And Tracy said she couldn't do it herself. She didn't have the — " The last word was drowned by laughter.

Now Lucy was laughing. "The what?"

"Tools!" Nora managed to say. "And Susan said. . . ."

Remembering Susan's comments about her belief that Tracy put up the picture herself, Jennifer doubled over with laughter.

". . . all she needed was a. . . ."

". . . tack!" Denise finished.

Tracy giggled. "I can just see it," she said.

The image of Tracy fixing her braces with tacks brought more laughter.

At the next table, Tommy Ryder, Mitch Pauley, and Jason Anthony sat gaping at the girls.

"What's their problem?" Mitch said.

"Somebody call an ambulance," Tommy said. "We have an emergency in the Cedar Groves cafeteria."

"Probably food poisoning," Jason joked.

Amy took deep breaths. Once more in control, she said, "Come on, you guys; let's show Tracy her picture."

"I can't wait to see it."

The girls snapped into action. They marched through the cafeteria, surrounding Tracy as though she were the President and they were the Secret Service. The boys fell into step behind them.

Tracy stopped abruptly. Jennifer had said the picture on the bulletin board in the front hall wasn't particularly good. She didn't want an audience of boys when she saw it. She ducked into the girls' room.

The other girls followed.

"You could've told us where you were going," Tommy said. "Save us a" — the door swung closed — "trip."

Inside, Lucy asked, "What's happening? I thought we were going to see your picture."

Tracy studied her image in the long mirror over the sinks. The big blue eyes, the pert nose, the rosy cheeks went unnoticed; it was as if her mouth, filled with silver braces, had grown to take up all the space. Pulling her lips tightly over her teeth, she said, "The bell's going to ring. I'll see it later."

Lucy was disappointed. She'd discovered the picture; she wanted to be there when Tracy saw it. "We'll make it if we hurry," she said.

Tracy smiled at her image. Her braces flashed in the light. "I can't face anybody." she said.

"Because of the picture?" Lucy asked.

Tracy shook her head. "The braces."

Denise was growing impatient. "Nobody even noticed the braces, Tracy; all they can think about is the picture." She started for the door. "I'm going to my locker. I'll see you all later," she said as she pushed through the door. The hall was empty. She poked her head back into the room. "If you're worried about an audience," she said to Tracy, "don't. Everyone's gone."

The girls piled out the door and crept down the hall, trying not to laugh and not to attract attention.

They reached the bulletin board as the bell rang, and raced off, leaving Tracy standing alone, her mouth open, her eyes wide — looking very much as she did in the picture with one important difference: the braces.

"Too bad we didn't see Tracy's reaction to the picture," Nora said as she got out the scalpel from the biology lab table drawer.

Jennifer opened her sketchbook. "The picture is sure getting a lot of attention."

"Today maybe," Denise said as she twisted her lab apron strings around her waist. "By tomorrow everybody will have forgotten about it."

"I'm not so sure," Nora said. "And I keep wondering how I'd feel. It's exciting and all that, but I don't think I'd want to be up there with everybody — "

Behind them a voice said, "Ever have the feeling you're being watched?"

They turned. Jason held two enormous cow eyes in front of his own.

"Jason! That is so gross!" Nora snapped.

Jennifer shivered. "Not half as gross as dissecting them."

From the front of the room, Mr. Morris directed, "Only one eye per table."

Jason dropped one cow eye into the dissecting pan on the table behind him. He placed the remaining eye in the center of his forehead as he hobbled back to his place.

Nora set to work on the dissection.

"I am so glad you're good at this, Nora," Denise said as she wrote their names at the top of the team's report sheet. "I keep wondering what would've happened if I'd been teamed with someone else."

Denise had transferred to Cedar Groves Junior High from a school in Switzerland at the beginning of the year, and Jennifer had offered to take her as a third lab partner. At first, Nora had resented her, but now she was as glad to have her as Jennifer was. They were a real team, with Nora doing the dissecting; Jennifer, the sketching; and Denise, the lab reports.

After school, Nora and Jennifer went

looking for Tracy. They found her in the front hall where they had left her.

"Don't tell me you've been here since lunch?" Nora said.

Without taking her eyes off her picture, Tracy shook her head. "No, but I couldn't get this picture out of my mind. Everybody kept talking about it, asking for my auto-graph — stuff like that."

"How do you feel about it?" Jennifer asked.

Tracy sighed. "That's the problem: I don't know how to feel."

"Why don't we go over to Temptations and talk about it," Nora suggested.

"That'd be great!" Tracy said. She hadn't eaten since breakfast. Her mouth still hurt. Maybe some soft, cold ice cream. . . .

Jennifer poked Nora. She had hoped Nora would come to her house, where the two of them could do a little homework and a lot of talking. She'd been so busy lately they'd hardly had any time to spend to-gether.

Nora didn't understand the message. "Do you have a meeting or something, Jen?"

Jennifer shook her head. "The only day this week I don't," she said pointedly.

"Great!" Nora said. "Then what are we waiting for?"

She and Tracy took off down the hall.

Sighing, Jennifer trailed along behind. Some days, she and Nora seemed able to read one another's minds. Today was obviously not one of them.

As the three of them threaded their way to the side door, people stopped digging in their lockers or talking to one another to stare at Tracy. The word *picture* floated in the air all around them.

"Hey, Trace!" someone called. "Can I have your autograph?"

"Hear that?" Nora said.

"I've been hearing it all afternoon," Tracy said.

"You're a celebrity!" Nora pointed out. "Nobody has had a picture *that* big on the bulletin board."

Tracy's lower lip jutted out. Some other day, that possibility might have pleased her, but not today.

Jennifer was quick to sense Tracy's feelings. "Don't pay any attention," she said. "Just smile."

Tracy looked at her helplessly. "I can't, she said. "My lips are stuck to my braces."

At the curb outside, Tony Hendrix, in his leather bomber jacket, lounged against the side of the family's BMW. With his black hair and dark eyes, he was extraordinarily handsome. He smiled when he saw Jennifer.

"Hi, Tony," Jennifer called down to him from the top of the stairs. Not too many weeks ago, seeing him — even at a distance — had brought such a big lump to her throat she had trouble talking to him. Then she had helped him get over a broken romance. In the process, she'd fallen madly in love with him and thought he'd felt the same way, despite the three years difference in their ages. When she found out he thought of her as a friend only, she had had mixed feelings. Now she was comfortable with their friendship. "Waiting for Denise?" she asked him.

Tony nodded. "But not patiently," he said. "Have you seen her?"

Although there was annoyance in his tone, Jennifer heard affection there, too. The family's many moves had built a particularly close relationship between Tony and Denise. "I think she's practicing a scene for drama club," Jennifer told him.

"How about waiting with me?" Tony suggested as the girls joined him at the curb. "I'll drive you all home."

Tracy liked that idea. Tony was the best-looking boy in the whole world. Her lips came unglued from her teeth. She smiled. Then, remembering her braces, she burrowed her face into the collar of her jacket and pulled her red scarf up around her mouth.

Tony didn't notice.

"Thanks," Nora said, "but we're not going home."

Just then, Denise came running down the stairs, hair flying. Full of apologies, she slid into the car. Tony ran around to the driver's side. They waved to the girls as they pulled away.

Tracy watched them with wide eyes. "Denise is so lucky to have him for a brother," she said.

Nora laughed. "A brother is the last thing I'd want him for."

Tracy thought about that for several seconds. Then she said seriously, "You know, you're right." She paused before adding, "Poor Denise."

As they left the protection of the building, the wind blew in their faces, taking their breath away. They huddled close for the push through the wind to Temptations.

Sliding into a corner booth, Tracy felt a sense of relief; none of their classmates was in the brass and glass decorated ice-cream parlor. She could eat without worrying about hiding her braces.

As Jennifer studied the menu, she said, "If I had to choose one kind of food to bring to a desert island," she said, "it would be a chocolate-marshmallow sundae from Temptations."

Nora laughed. "If you've said that once, you've said it a thousand times."

Tracy looked up over the large menu, her eyes wide. "A person can never say a true thing like that too often."

Nora gave her a sidelong glance. Sometimes she had a hard time believing Tracy was for real. How could anybody take everything so literally?

After they gave their orders, Jennifer said, "That's settled. Now let's talk about your picture, Trace. You said you didn't know how to feel — right?"

Tracy nodded.

"That's the way I was with Tony," Jennifer continued. "I mean I wanted to be his 'girl friend,' you know? And at first when I knew he just wanted to be friends, I didn't know how to feel."

"I wouldn't have trouble with that one," Tracy said. "I'd know how to feel: rotten!"

They laughed. Then, growing serious again, Nora said, "It wasn't that you didn't know how to feel, Jen; you just didn't know what you were *already* feeling. There's a difference."

"But if a person's feeling lots of different things," Jennifer countered, "she has to — "

"That's it!" Tracy interrupted. She sounded triumphant, as though she'd just figured out the answer to a difficult puzzle.

"That's ex*act*ly what I'm feeling."

They turned to look at her expectantly. When Tracy made no move to elaborate, Nora said, "So? What are you feeling, Trace?"

Tracy sighed. She thought she'd been perfectly clear.

"Tracy means she's feeling lots of different things," Jennifer explained. "Isn't that right, Trace?"

Tracy nodded. "Right."

"Like what?" Nora persisted.

"That's what I have to decide," Tracy said.

"That's my whole point, Tracy," Nora said patiently. "A person can't just *decide* how to feel; she just feels."

Tracy looked puzzled.

"Maybe what we should do is make a list," Jennifer suggested as she dug her notebook out of the bookbag beside her. "We'll put the good things about having your picture on the bulletin board in one column and the bad things in another."

"That sounds good," Tracy said. Then she didn't say anything.

With pen poised over the blank sheet of paper, Jennifer waited.

"Aren't you going to write anything?" Tracy asked at last.

"You have to tell me what to write," Jennifer said.

"Oh," Tracy said. Her face was pinched in thought. "Like what?" she said after a few minutes.

"Let's start with the good. Did the picture do anything that made you feel good?"

"One thing," Tracy began hesitantly, "it kept everybody from noticing my braces."

Jennifer began to write.

"That's also bad," Tracy added, "because if everybody'd noticed the braces today, it'd be all over with: I'd know what they were going to say; now I have to go through all the agony of waiting to find out all over again."

Nora shook her head. "I don't think this is going to work, Jen."

Just then, a burst of air announced Mia's arrival. She stood in the open doorway, scanning the place behind rhinestone sunglasses. Her rainbow-spiked hair was bent at odd angles. She spotted the girls and made for their booth.

"Anybody see Andy?" she asked as she slid in beside Jennifer.

Tracy said, "Last time I saw him was — "

" — at lunchtime," Nora interrupted. To be exact, they had last seen him in the front hall studying Tracy's picture. Judging by the way Mia had reacted this morning, she wouldn't be too happy to hear that.

Mia drummed her long electric-blue fingernails on the Formica tabletop. "I don't know what I'm going to do about him," she said. "He's getting awfully peculiar lately."

At the same time, Nora and Jennifer thought *Lately?* as they exchanged amused glances.

Mia sighed and opened the domed metal lunchbox she used as a purse. She rummaged around in it, finally extracting a can of mousse. She shook it. "Empty. Anybody got any mousse?"

No one did.

"Now what'll I do? I can't sit here and have a sundae without mousse."

Tracy blinked twice. "Wouldn't you rather have whipped cream?"

"Ha-ha. Very funny," Mia said. "For my *hair*. I have to do something with it. It's a mess."

Nora choked back a giggle. "No one'd know," she said.

"You and your preppy look," Mia responded. "You have no idea how difficult it is to keep up an image like mine."

"You could cut it off — be bald," Jennifer teased.

"Never!" Mia said. "A woman's hair is her crowning glory."

Nora and Jennifer avoided looking at one another. If their eyes met, they knew they'd dissolve in laughter.

Mia turned to Tracy. "Did you put that picture up on the bulletin board like Susan said?"

Her directness made Jennifer squirm.

But Tracy met Mia's gaze. "I don't even know who *took* it!" she said.

Jennifer and Nora stared at Tracy in disbelief. Until now, they had thought only of the photo itself and of Tracy's reactions to it. It had never occurred to them to wonder who took it. That Tracy didn't know came as a great shock. "You don't know who took it?" they said in unison.

Mia whistled between her teeth. "Taking your picture and putting it up on the bulletin board like that — whoever it is must like you."

Tracy lowered her eyes. "Not enough to ask me if it was okay first," she said.

Chapter 4

Nora was playing with Sinbad, her pet hamster, when the telephone rang. She put the animal into his cage and reached for the phone. "Hi, Jen," she said.

On the other end of the line, Jennifer put down her Things To Do list and leaned back against her pink pillows. "How'd you know it was me?"

"Who else?" Nora said. They had talked on the phone at the same time every night for as long as she could remember.

"Oh, I don't know," Jennifer teased. "Maybe Brad Hartley."

Brad was in Nora's shop class. After the class trip to Washington, D.C., in the fall, he had taken her out for pizza and a movie — her first real date. Since then, although he always smiled when he saw her, he had not asked her out. Nora wasn't surprised even though she would have liked it if he'd taken her out again. But except for Mia and Andy, their crowd went places as a group.

"Don't I wish," Nora said. After a brief pause during which she imagined Brad's handsome face smiling at her, she said, "Did you finish your homework?"

"All but the problem of the week," Jennifer said. "I did it, but I don't think it's right."

Nora turned in her desk chair and caught a glimpse of her open closet and the sweaters inside, arranged neatly on three shelves according to color and texture. "What're you going to wear tomorrow?"

"I don't know," Jennifer said. "Probably the T-shirt you gave me." The shirt had been a present the Christmas before. It read: SO MUCH TO DO . . . SO LITTLE TIME. "I really need some new clothes."

"Do you have any money?"

"Some. Baby-sitting and allowance. I've been saving."

"Let's go shopping Saturday," Nora suggested.

"Can't. I've got the animal shelter in the morning and then we're canvassing the neighborhood for contributions for Save the Whales."

"Maybe they could throw in some old clothes with their contributions. You're always so busy, you'll never have time to shop."

Jennifer laughed. "That's an idea."

"Kill two birds with one stone, as they say," Nora added.

"Never!" Jennifer said.

"I'm talking *mythical* birds," Nora explained. "They're not on the endangered list."

They both laughed. Although Jennifer was serious about trying to do what she could to save not only whales but any endangered species, she didn't mind a little teasing on the subject. Especially tonight. She was beginning to feel pressured by her commitments, and it relieved the tension to have Nora joke about them.

"Speaking of which," Nora continued, "what about Tracy?"

"Endangered? Tracy? Never. She could survive anything."

"I don't know, Jen. I'd be pretty upset if someone took my picture without telling me and hung it up in school. Who do you think did it?"

"I'm still trying to figure out *how* anyone could do it. I mean, I'd know, wouldn't you?"

Nora hadn't thought about that before. "Photographers can be pretty tricky," she said. "They've got all those long lenses and things. Movie stars and people are always complaining about them."

"Professional photographers, maybe,

but whoever took Tracy's picture has to be somebody from school; otherwise it wouldn't have turned up on the bulletin board. Who's got that kind of equipment? And why would they want to take her picture without telling her, anyway?"

"Maybe it's somebody with a crush on her, and he wants to get her attention."

"Every boy in the class has Tracy's attention already."

Nora had to agree to the truth of that.

"The way I figure it," Jennifer went on, "Tracy must've forgotten who took it or something."

"Even so," Nora said, "I'd sure like to find out who it was."

"Why?" Jennifer said. "The picture'll probably be gone tomorrow. And then Tracy'll *know* how to feel: disappointed because she's not getting all the attention."

Nora hugged the pink calico cat pillow Jennifer had made for her birthday. She was surprised at her friend's reaction. Jennifer was always so protective of Tracy. Nora sensed there was something more going on than they realized. And she was worried about Tracy. Yet, where people's feelings were concerned, Jennifer's instincts were right on target. She's probably right, Nora thought. I'm making too big a thing of it.

* * *

Next morning when Nora and Jen arrived at school, Jason Anthony was sitting alone on the front steps, his red hair gleaming in the morning light.

"Where is everybody?" Nora asked him.

Intent on pushing the end of a bent coat hanger down between his cast and his leg, he didn't respond.

"You shouldn't do that," Nora said. "You'll ruin your cast."

"And if I don't do it, my leg'll fall off from itching."

"That's impossible," Nora said. "Just think about something else and it'll stop itching."

Jason stopped scratching and looked up at her. "Like what?"

"How should I know, Jason?" Nora said. When she became a doctor, she hoped she'd never have *him* for a patient. "Your skateboard or something."

After a moment's silence, he moaned and doubled over.

"*Now* what's the matter?"

"I was thinking about my skateboard."

"So?"

"It's making me sick to my stomach — "

"Join the crowd," Jennifer said lightly.

" — because Mr. Donovan still has it," Jason finished.

Tired of the conversation, Nora looked

around. "Where is everybody?" she repeated.

"Inside," Jason said. "Something about Tracy's picture."

Jennifer and Nora exchanged puzzled glances. Then they dashed up the stairs.

The front hall was deserted as the two of them ran to the main bulletin board. Tracy's picture was gone.

Jennifer nodded smugly. "What'd I tell you?"

Mr. Mario appeared suddenly. "Signing up for camera club?" he asked. The club was his idea.

"Haven't decided," Nora said.

He tacked a blank piece of paper under the filled sign-up sheet. Then he stood back. "Something's missing."

"Tracy's picture," Jennifer offered.

The man nodded. "Oh, yes. Interesting work. Who took it?"

The girls shrugged.

Andy Warwick came up beside him. "Hi, Mr. Mario," he said cheerfully.

Mr. Mario gave him the once over, shook his head, and drifted off.

Andy looked hurt. "That man has *never* liked me," he muttered.

"Where is everybody?" Nora asked Andy.

He jerked his thumb over his shoulder.

"When they found out Tracy's picture was gone, they probably went to the cafeteria or somewhere," Jennifer concluded.

Nora started down the hall. "Let's find out."

Ahead, Tracy rounded the corner surrounded by a group of boys. They jostled one another, trying for the positions closest to her.

Tommy Ryder broke from the others and skipped ahead of her. "Tracy," he said, "if you'd just listen. . . ."

Tracy walked with her head high and her eyes straight ahead, as though she were unaware of the commotion. As she approached Nora and Jennifer, she smiled weakly. "Am I glad to see you," she said.

"What's going on?" Nora asked.

"Don't ask me. When I got to school, everybody was inside so I came in, too, and then these . . . creeps. . . ." Her voice quavered.

The boys all started talking at once. Tommy's voice overrode the others. "We've been trying to tell you, Tracy — your picture — "

" — is gone from the bulletin board," Nora said. "So what else is new?"

"Not that one," Mitch said. "There's another one. We'd like to know what's going on, but Tracy won't tell us anything."

Tracy stamped her foot. "How could I tell you anything?" she croaked. "I don't even know what you're talking about."

"Where's this other picture?" Nora asked.

Saying, "Follow me," Tommy turned on his heel and headed toward the eighth grade lockers.

Along the way, other classmates joined the procession.

"Where are we going?" Susan Hillard asked.

"To see Tracy's picture," Jennifer told her.

Susan dropped back. "You're going the wrong — "

The group turned a corner. They picked up their pace, sweeping whoever was in their path along with them. At the lockers, Tommy Ryder stopped abruptly. Everybody piled into him. He silenced their grumbling with upraised hands. Then, saying, "Ta-da!" he indicated the bulletin board reserved for student messages with a sweep of his arm.

Covering the entire board was a picture of Tracy Douglas, wearing the same bewildered expression as she had in the first picture. But this time, she wasn't alone: Standing beside her, gazing at her, was Jason Anthony.

Nora shot a glance at Tracy. Momentarily dazed, Tracy suddenly drew herself to her full height and silently slipped away. One of the boys noticed her escape, sounded the alarm, and the boys trooped after her.

Mitch Pauley hung back, shaking his head. "Jason Anthony?" he said, reluctant to believe what he saw.

Studying the picture, Lucy said, "If I didn't know better, I'd think this and yesterday's picture were the same."

"Tracy wasn't with anybody in the other one," Amy said.

"And the other was a head and shoulders shot," Mia put in. "This one's full-length."

"But the expression is exactly the same," Lucy pointed out.

The bell rang.

Everyone turned as one and rushed back along the hall, branching off in small groups toward their various homerooms.

Susan joined the flow at the first juncture. "What'd I tell you?" she said to Nora and Jennifer. "You were going the wrong way."

The two friends turned into room 332.

"Tracy's picture is outside the gym," Susan added as she moved on.

Nora and Jennifer looked at each other and darted back into the hall.

"What did you say?" Nora called, but Susan had disappeared.

"A third picture?" Jennifer exclaimed. "She must be kidding!"

Behind them, a voice said, "Ladies, are you joining us this morning or are you waiting for an engraved invitation?"

Mr. Mario stood with his hand on the doorknob, ready to close the door. Jennifer smiled sheepishly as she and Nora slid past him and headed for their seats, side-stepping Jason's cast as they scrambled down the aisle.

"Watch it," Jason said as he drew in the injured leg.

In her seat, Nora turned to question him about the picture.

"Ms. Ryan," Mr. Mario said wearily, "now that you're here, may we please have your whole attention?"

Nora faced front. Great. Now Mr. Mario'd be watching her the whole home-room period, and she wouldn't have a chance to talk to Jason.

The door opened and Denise came in, a silver bag from the most expensive store in town balanced on top of her books. She handed Mr. Mario an admit slip.

"What's in the bag?" Nora whispered as Denise passed by.

Denise tipped the bag to reveal a piece of something black and fuzzy. Nora recognized it as a wig. Costume, she identified to herself. Denise belonged to the drama club, and they were doing scenes that afternoon.

Through the rest of the homeroom period, Nora kept her eyes on the clock over Mr. Mario's head. The hands seemed frozen. Finally, she heard the whirr that preceded the bell. She swiveled toward Jason.

"Ms. Ryan," Mr. Mario said, "a famous sports figure once said, 'The game's not over till it's over.' The same goes for home — "

The bell rang.

Mr. Mario shrugged. "Go for it," he said.

The expression was so uncharacteristic of the man it stunned Nora. By the time she recovered, Jason was leaving the room.

I'll just have to talk to Tracy about the picture, Nora thought. But for the next three periods, that was impossible, too. Before each class, Tracy's desk was surrounded by boys; between classes, they escorted her from room to room. She sure was a celebrity!

Fourth period, Nora found Jennifer in front of the bulletin board outside the gym.

"Susan wasn't kidding," Jennifer said. "Here's the third picture."

Nora's jaw dropped. She gaped at Tracy's image, which stared back, looking equally bewildered. The girl was alone on this picture as she had been in the first. "I can't believe it," she said.

Denise walked past, stopping at the locker room door to ask, "Is there anything on that board I should know about?"

"Tracy's picture," Jennifer said.

Denise steadied her books and the silver bag with her chin and reached to open the door. "Is that all? I thought maybe gym was canceled. I could sure use the extra time to practice my part for this afternoon."

"Denise," Nora said impatiently, "aren't you even interested? Something's going on here. Since yesterday there've been a total of *three* pictures!"

Andy Warwick passed behind them saying, "Four. There's one in the boys' locker room."

By the time it took that bit of information to seep in, Tracy and her all-male escort were approaching from the other direction. Tracy was smiling broadly.

Susan appeared at Jennifer's elbow. "What'd I tell you?" she gloated. "Little Miss Boy-Crazy is getting *exactly* what she wanted."

At the door to the girls' locker room, Tracy turned to the boys. "Sorry, no boys allowed," she said sweetly. Then she stuck out her tongue and darted inside.

The girls piled in after her. Tracy's sunny smile had disappeared under a dark cloud of anger.

"They are *such* creeps!" she said as she threw open her locker door. "All that smiling — my face actually hurts from smiling — and do you think one of them even noticed?" Without waiting for an answer, she hastened to add, "No, of course not. All they can think about is those stupid pictures. Something really important like braces and nobody notices!" She thrust a leg into her shapeless blue gym shorts. "Boys are so . . . so . . . trivial!"

Chapter 5

Boys are trivial? Was this Tracy Douglas speaking? The girls looked at each other, too shocked to laugh.

Nora opened her mouth to speak; what came out was a weak, "Trivial . . . ?"

At that moment, Tracy angrily pulled open her locker door, making too much noise to hear.

Nora cleared her throat and began again. "I thought you didn't want anyone to notice your braces, Tracy." She slipped into her gym shorts.

"That was yesterday," Tracy said, "before those stupid boys decided to follow me everywhere."

"My mother always says be careful what you ask for," Susan Hillard said smugly, "'cause you might get it."

Tracy turned on her. "I never asked for you to be so mean to me," she snapped, "but you always are."

Susan flinched. Tracy had never before spoken up to her like that. Usually, she caved in in the face of Susan's barbs. Unable to think of a comeback, Susan turned on her heel and marched toward the gym.

"Way to go, Trace," Lucy said.

Tracy slammed her locker door. "Why is she always like that?"

"Don't pay attention," Jennifer advised.

"Some people are just nasty," Nora added. "It's a chemical imbalance or something."

"Besides, it always backfires," Lucy said about Susan's behavior.

They all agreed.

"Just the same," Tracy said as she headed for the gym, "I don't like it."

After gym, Tracy peeked out into the hall and saw Tommy and Mitch waiting for her. She listened to what they were saying.

"If we just keep close to her, one of us will be in the next picture with her," Tommy said. "*And* on a bulletin board."

"Yeah, that's why every guy in school is following her," Mitch said. "We're not the only ones."

Tracy slammed the door and stood against it. "They're out there! What'll I do?"

Lucy pulled her oversized peach sweater over her head. "Don't panic, Trace. I'll just go out first and tell them you've already gone."

Tracy stepped away from the door to let Lucy pass. "Would you?"

"Wait here," Lucy said. "I'll let you know when the coast is clear." She flung upon the door and waltzed out. "If you're waiting for Tracy," she told the boys, "she's gone."

His glance fixed on a spot over her shoulder, Tommy snorted. "Then who's that?"

Lucy turned just as the door behind her closed on Tracy's frozen smile. "My mistake," Lucy said sheepishly as she backed into the locker room. Inside, she shook her head. "I do *not* believe you, Tracy Douglas," she said. "How could you do that?"

Tracy watched her foot making circles on the worn tile floor. "You didn't give me time to get away from the door," she said. "Now what'll I do?"

"You could stay until the bell rings," Jennifer suggested.

"Pretend to be sick. Then you can go to the nurse's office," Nora offered. She gave that a second thought, then added, "On your way, tell those creeps off."

Jennifer disagreed. "That'd make things worse. She should ignore them." She turned to Denise, who stood in front of her locker, mumbling to herself. "What d'you think, Denise?"

Denise slipped her foot into her penny loafer and looked blankly at Jennifer.

"The boys are waiting outside for Tracy and she doesn't know what to do," Jennifer explained.

Denise shrugged. "I've got my own problems." She held up a sheaf of papers. "A scene in *Romeo and Juliet*. I have to *die* this afternoon, and I don't even know the lines!" She scooped up her books and the silver bag she'd carried with her all morning.

"I'm *already* dead," Tracy moaned. She sank to a bench and dropped her chin into her hands. "I can't even think with those creeps following me everywhere."

That was too much for Susan. Shaking her head, she left the room.

"If only I could be . . . somebody else. . . ." Tracy's voice trailed off sadly.

"That's it!" Nora said. "Tracy, you're a genius!"

Tracy blinked. "A genius?" She looked around to be sure Nora wasn't talking to someone else. "Me?"

Nora snatched Denise's bag from on top of her books.

"Nora, give me that," Denise protested. "It's my costume!"

Nora pulled out the dark wig. "I know."

She smiled wickedly. "And it's just what the doctor ordered." She plopped the wig on Tracy's head.

As understanding of Nora's plan dawned on the others one by one, they began talking all at once.

Tracy alone remained in the dark. "What are you doing?" she sputtered.

"I am your fairy godmother come to grant your wish," Nora said as she adjusted the wig.

Tracy looked from one to the other.

"What wish? I didn't make any wish."

Nora stepped back to admire her handiwork. "If you can't leave here as Tracy Douglas," she said, "you'll leave as — "

The light snapped on in Tracy's eyes. " — someone else?" she said. She shook her head slowly. "I can't do that. How can I do that?"

"What'll she wear?" Lucy asked. "They'll recognize her sweater."

Denise extracted an ankle-length black taffeta skirt and a ruffled white blouse from her bag. "Here's the rest of my costume," she said, sighing with resignation.

Tracy's eyes lit up. She reached for the skirt. "That is *so* pretty!"

Nora snatched it. "She can't wear this!"

Tracy's mouth drooped. "Why not?"

"Tracy, you can't go out there looking like Cathy from *Wuthering Heights*," Jennifer explained. "You have to pass as an eighth-grade girl, or the boys'll know."

"*Which* eighth-grade girl?" she asked.

"Tra*cy*!" Jennifer was losing patience.

"She's right, Jen," Nora said. "The boys know all the girls. She can't look like nobody; she has to look like somebody."

"You mean like one of us?" Lucy asked, intrigued.

Nora nodded. "Otherwise, it won't work."

"No matter what we do, Tracy won't look like any of us," Jennifer said. "And if she did, then there'd be two of one of us."

"Not if the original stays here till the boys are gone," Nora said. "I mean Tracy's not going to *stay* that person."

Tracy parted the dark hair hanging over her eyes. "Which person?"

"Well," Nora began, her glance sliding from one to the other. "You and Susan are the same height."

Tracy shot to her feet. "I will *not* be Susan Hillard!"

"Besides, Susan already left," Lucy pointed out. "The boys must've seen her."

Nora nodded. "How about Amy? Where is she?"

"Inside helping Mrs. Scott put away equipment," Lucy said.

"She wouldn't work anyway," Jennifer

said. "She and Tracy aren't built anything alike."

"Lucy!" Nora said. "Tracy's taller than you, but if she squinches down. . . ."

"Nora," Lucy said, shaking her head. "In case you haven't noticed, I'm black and Tracy's white."

"How about you, Nora?" Jennifer asked. "This whole thing was your idea."

"It wasn't mine," Nora protested. "It was Tracy's."

Tracy pulled off the wig. "Mine? I don't even know what's happening!"

Nora ignored that. "Besides, my hair's practically as short as Lucy's."

Denise sighed. "She can't be me! I'm a blonde!!"

They all looked at Jennifer.

Jennifer backed away. "Oh, no. Not me. It'd never work."

Her hands on her hips, Nora moved toward her friend. "Of course it'll work. The wig's exactly the same color as your hair, and we can tie it back into a ponytail."

Backed into a corner, Jennifer challenged, "I'm way taller than Tracy. What're you going to do about that?"

"She can . . . stand on tiptoe," Nora suggested.

Tracy muttered, "I don't think I can do this."

"Come on, Jen, take off your T-shirt," Nora urged.

"Couldn't she wear someone else's clothes?"

"Not if she's going to be you."

Mumbling her objections, Jennifer slipped out of her T-shirt. "What am *I* going to wear?"

Nora looked at Tracy.

Reluctantly, Tracy handed over her pink angora sweater.

"Be careful with this T-shirt," Jennifer cautioned. It was her SO MUCH TO DO . . . T-shirt, and she hated parting with it. She slipped Tracy's sweater over her head. Several inches of skin showed between the bottom of it and the waistband of her purple jeans. "Look at this!" she exclaimed. "I can't wear this!"

"Take mine," Lucy said as she struggled out of her sweater. "It's extra long."

"And it's peach!" Jennifer objected. "I'll clash!"

"Mine'll go," Nora offered. "Yellow and purple are good together."

Jennifer made a sour face.

Half out of her sweater, Nora fixed her glance on Denise's shirt. It was a soft lavender.

Denise shook her head "Not a chance."

"So take this, Jen," Nora said, thrusting her sweater at her friend. "It's only for a little while. And I'll take Lucy's and Lucy can wear Tracy's." She poked her head through Lucy's sweater. "Tracy. . . ." She looked around. "Where's Tracy?"

"By the mirror," Tracy responded. She stepped around the bank of lockers on tiptoe, the wig firmly on her head. "Will I pass?" She smiled wanly; her braces flashed.

"If you don't smile," Nora said. She moved close to Tracy, motioning Lucy and Denise to do the same. "What we've got to do is keep Tracy sort of in the middle so no one gets a really good look at her."

Denise and Lucy took up positions on either side of Tracy. Nora took the lead. As they moved toward the door, Nora looked over her shoulder. "This isn't going to work," she said. "We need somebody behind Tracy."

Tracy glanced around. "What about Jen?"

"Tracy," Lucy said, "*you* are Jen!"

Tracy burrowed her head into her shoulders, tipping the wig forward. "I forgot."

Behind them, a voice said, "What's going on?"

Amy stood at the door to the gym.

"Tell you later," Nora said. "Quick! Get behind Tracy."

Amy complied, following along to the locker room door.

Nora cracked open the door. The hall was empty.

"Are they out there?" Lucy asked.

Nora shook her head.

On tiptoe, Tracy peered over her shoulder. "I'll bet they're waiting around the corner."

"You're going out *there*?" Amy said. "I can't go out *there*! I'm in gym clothes!"

Tracy craned her neck to get a better view of the hall. "It doesn't matter whose clothes you're in," she said. "I'm in Jennifer's and she's in Nora's and Nora's in Lucy's and Lucy's in mine. So if you're in Jim's — "

Amy's breath escaped in a high-pitched hiss. "I don't believe this!"

"Wait here, Jen; I'll come back for you," Nora instructed.

Tracy stiffened. "Nora, let's not do this. I don't want to — "

Nora grabbed Tracy's wrist and pulled her out into the hall.

The girls moved down the hall as one. Tracy, on tiptoe, bobbed up and down between them. They rounded the corner cautiously. This corridor, too, was empty except for Andy Warwick, who was coming toward them, a toothpick between his lips.

"Where is everybody?" Nora asked him.

Andy rolled the toothpick to the side of his mouth. "Lunch."

"Lunch?" Lucy said. "The bell didn't even ring."

"Maybe not for you," he said. "For everybody else it rang fifteen minutes ago." As he passed, he said, "Hey, Tracy, Tommy and Mitch've been looking for you."

Mitch and Tommy cornered Jason when he came into the cafeteria.

"Where've you been all morning?" Mitch wanted to know.

"Here," Jason said.

"We didn't see you," Tommy said.

"Of course not," Jason countered. "You've been too busy following Tracy around."

"And you haven't, I suppose," Mitch said.

Jason blew on his fingernails and rubbed them on the lapel of his camouflage jacket. "*I* don't have to."

Tommy and Mitch looked very jealous.

Jason relished their reaction to his short response. He didn't even have to mention the picture. After all, it showed him standing next to Tracy Douglas. The fact that he couldn't remember ever having been close enough to the girl alone to have had his picture taken with her didn't matter. If, as Susan said, Tracy was responsible for the pictures, then she must like him. So, the less said the better. Let them draw their own conclusions. Besides, the picture was not tops on his priority list; getting his skateboard back was.

Tommy whipped out his pocket comb and ran it through his sandy brown hair. "Something's wrong," he said. "*I'm* the one who should be in that picture with Tracy."

"Hey, hey," Mitch said, as he squared his shoulders and made fists at his sides, "it's *my* picture that should be up there."

"With Tracy?" Jason asked.

"*My* picture," Mitch growled. "Me, alone. There was a picture of me on the bulletin board in the front hall and on the one in the boys' locker room. Now they're both gone."

"Now I get it," Jason said. "You're following her to be sure she doesn't replace any more of your pictures?"

Andy came up silently and stood at Tommy's elbow, listening.

Tommy sighed. "I'm following her so that I'm there the next time she has her picture taken. Tracy's crazy about me. If she's going around having her picture taken, I'm the one that should be in the picture with her."

"You're wasting your time; that's not the way it's done," Andy said and swaggered off.

Tommy whirled. "Hey, Warwick! What's that supposed to mean?" he asked, but Andy was already out of earshot.

"It's obvious," Jason said. "Andy means following Tracy around isn't the way to get her attention. You'll never be 'in the picture' with any girl, Ryder, if you keep acting like a jerk."

Tommy chortled. "Look who's talking."

Outside the girls' room, Denise snatched the wig off Tracy's head. "I don't know how I ever got involved in this." She stuffed the wig into her silver bag, said, "I should be practicing my scene," and marched off toward the cafeteria.

The other girls ducked into the girls' lounge.

Tracy yanked Jennifer's T-shirt over her head. "Give me my sweater, Lucy." Her voice hovered between rage and frustration.

"You don't have to snap my head off, Tracy," Lucy said as she struggled out of the pink sweater. "This wasn't my idea, you know." She turned to Nora. "Give me my sweater, Nora."

"Now, *you're* snapping at *me!*" Nora said.

"*You* deserve it!" Lucy snatched her sweater from Nora and popped it over her head. "Come on, Tracy," she said. She and Tracy stuck their noses in the air and sailed out of the room.

"Hey, wait a minute!" Nora called after them. "What'll I wear?" She scooped Jennifer's T-shirt off the floor. "My choices are definitely limited," she said as she dropped it over her head. Then she dashed out of the room.

She caught up with Lucy and Tracy at the cafeteria counter.

"At least there's no line," Nora said, trying to ease the tension.

"No food, either," Lucy said.

The bell rang.

"And no time to eat it," Tracy said sadly.

Jennifer tore down the hall after Nora, who was racing toward her locker. "Nora!" she called. "Wait up!"

Nora stopped dead.

Jennifer skidded to a stop. "I waited like you said, and you never came back. Where were you? Where's Tracy? And what are you doing in my T-shirt?" She was too angry to wait for answers. "Really, Nora Ryan, sometimes it's very hard to be your friend. I missed lunch and it's all your fault. And you were going to show me how you did the problem of the week and — "

"Problem of the *week*?" Nora exploded. "I can't even handle the problem of the *minute*!"

Chapter 6

After school, Mia found Jason leaning against the wall outside Mr. Donovan's office, his arms crossed over his chest. "Have you seen Andy?" she asked him.

"He's probably with Mitch and Tommy."

"Why would he be with those jerks?" Mia was ready for an argument.

Jason wasn't. He just wanted to be left alone to wait for Mr. Donovan. He missed his skateboard and was ready to take any punishment to get it back. He shrugged. "You're right. He wouldn't be with them. He's probably with Tracy."

Mia planted her short sturdy legs far apart. With her leopard print tights and the halo of spiked hair around her face, she looked like a cat about to pounce. "Tracy!? Have you totally lost it!?"

Jason sighed. "I only know what I hear."

"And what's that?"

"Andy said something about knowing how to get Tracy's attention, that's all."

Mia began to pace.

"Actually what he said was 'That's not how it's done.' He was talking to Tommy and Mitch, and they were talking about following Tracy around and — "

Mia took out a tube of body streaker and, continuing to pace, ran an iridescent line up each forearm.

"War paint?" Jason asked. When Mia turned on him, he held up his hands as if surrendering. "Maybe he was talking about something else," he said. "I wasn't really listening."

"Where *is* Tracy?" Mia demanded.

Jason shrugged. "Find one, you find the other."

Mia growled. "Why am I standing here talking to you, Jason Anthony?"

"I've been asking myself that very same question. Between the two of us, we should be able to come up with an answer."

Mia stalked off.

Inside the girls' room, Nora said, "Tracy, you can't stay here all afternoon."

Tracy worked a small square of wax into a narrow band. "Why not?" She leaned toward the mirror over the sinks.

"Maybe *she* can," Jennifer said at the

door, "but I can't. You coming, Nora, or what?"

"Come on, Trace," Nora urged. "Everyone's gone by now."

As Tracy pressed the wax against the sides of her top braces, she said, "Go ahead without me," but it was garbled.

Nora shot Jennifer a questioning glance.

"Don't look at me," Jennifer said. "I can't translate."

Tracy fixed their images in the mirror. "I said, 'Go ahead without me.' "

Nora objected. "But Tracy — "

"See you, Tracy," Jennifer said, and she was out the door.

"Jennifer!" Nora looked helplessly at Tracy, who was busy pressing wax over her bottom braces. "You're sure you don't want me to wait?"

Tracy said something Nora didn't understand. At the same time, she nodded her head. Was that a "yes, go" or a "yes, wait"?

Nora's shoulders drooped indecisively. Stay or go? Finally, she edged toward the door. "If you're sure. . . ."

Alternately smiling at her image and readjusting the wax, Tracy didn't respond.

Nora was out the door and down the hall. "Have you seen Jen?" she asked Jason, who sat on the floor outside the office, his cast straight out in front of him.

"Everybody's looking for somebody," he said.

Mia found Tommy and Mitch outside the front entrance.

"Where's Andy?" she demanded.

Tommy whipped out his comb as she approached. "Haven't seen him."

Tossing a basketball from hand to hand, Mitch said, "We're looking for Tracy. You seen her?"

Mia sank down to the top step. "Find one," she said, "you find the other."

Denise came into the girls' room wearing the long skirt and ruffled blouse. She held the wig in her hand. "Am I glad that's over," she said to Tracy.

Tracy deposited the small envelope containing her wax into her bag. "How'd it go?"

"Terrible," Denise said. "Mrs. Hogan said I overplayed. Believe me, dying is not as easy as it looks."

"Especially without experience," Tracy said.

"Right," Denise said uncertainly. Then she went on, "On top of everything, I'm late. Tony's probably out in the parking lot, having a fit." A thought struck her. "Are you waiting for somebody, Tracy?"

For everybody to leave, Tracy thought. She said, "Sort of."

"Would you do me a big favor? Would you go outside and tell Tony I'll be there just as soon as I change?"

Tracy glanced at the clock. Four-thirty. Surely everyone would have gone by now. "I guess so," she said.

"You're a lifesaver," Denise said. "And if anybody comes looking for you, I'll tell them you're outside."

"No, don't do that!" Tracy sounded stricken. "If anybody asks, you haven't seen me."

This was getting more confusing by the second. "Whatever you say," Denise said.

Tracy peeked around the door. The hall in both directions was deserted. Hugging the wall, she crept toward the side door. Once there, she opened it a crack and peered out. Tony stood at the foot of the stairs with his back to her. She started out. Tommy, Mitch, and Mia rounded the corner at the front of the building. Tracy scampered back inside and closed the door. She heard Tony call, "Have you guys seen Denise?" Their answer was muffled by the sound of running feet.

When everything was quiet again, Tracy opened the door just wide enough to look out. Tony was pacing the sidewalk beside the BMW. She opened the door a bit wider.

The others were not in sight. She slid through the door and ran down the steps to Tony's side.

"Denise said you should wait; she'll be here just as soon as she changes," she said in one big rush.

Tony laughed. "Slow down, Tracy. You sound like you're being chased."

"I am!"

Just then, Mia, Mitch, and Tommy appeared at the back of the building near the athletic field fence.

"Quick! Hide me!" Tracy exclaimed as she moved closer to Tony.

Automatically, Tony dropped his arm around Tracy's shoulder as he glanced behind him. With the trio bearing down on them, he reached out, opened the passenger side of his car, and helped Tracy in. "Always ready to help a lady in distress," he said and dashed around to the driver's side.

Seeing them, Mia stopped dead.

Mitch tried to stop, but Tommy plowed into him and forced him into Mia.

Mia took several running steps to regain her balance. Then she spun to face the boys. "Watch it!" she shouted.

"It wasn't my fault," Mitch defended.

Keeping her eyes on the boys, Mia began to run. "Come on, before she gets away!"

Tommy took off after her. Mitch hung

back, scratching his head. "Before who gets away?"

Mia faced front. Tony's car was gone. She stopped short.

Tommy plowed into her. "You oughta be equipped with brake lights," he said.

Denise burst through the door and vaulted down the steps. "Has anyone seen Tony?" she asked Mia and the boys.

"He was here a minute ago," Mitch said.

Mia sighed. "Find Tracy and you find Tony."

The others gaped at her questioningly.

Nora couldn't find Jennifer anywhere. By the time she gave up the search, she was really annoyed. For a person who was supposed to be so sensitive and caring, Jen was certainly acting peculiarly. She seemed reluctant to help Tracy and impatient with Nora's interest. It didn't make sense. Sure, she was busy, but helping others was what Jen was all about — the *reason* she was so busy.

Absorbed in her thoughts, Nora went out the front entrance, down the stairs, and up the walk.

"Hi, Nora," someone said.

Several feet later, the greeting registered. Brad Hartley!

Her heart skipped. Her face went red hot. Smiling, she turned back to look up into the boy's clear blue eyes. "Brad, hi," she said, trying to sound casual. "I didn't . . . uh . . . see you." That sounded so dumb. And, in one sense, untrue: She saw him everywhere — even in her dreams.

He smiled warmly. "Probably didn't recognize me with *this* over my face." He held up a camera.

"Taking pictures?" she asked. That sounded dumb, too. What else would he be doing with a camera?

"A few," he answered. "Kind of practicing."

"Practicing?"

"I thought I'd join the camera club."

"Really? I've been thinking about joining, too," she said.

"That's great," he said.

Then they just stood there smiling at one another.

It wasn't until each had gone his separate way that Nora felt things click into focus.

"Brad Hartley has a camera!" she said to Jennifer over the phone that night.

"So?" Jennifer said.

"He takes pictures!"

Jennifer sighed heavily. "That's what people do with cameras, Nora."

"What I mean is do you think he's . . . the one?"

None of this was making sense. "The one?"

"The one taking Tracy's picture," Nora explained impatiently.

Trying to organize the puzzle pieces into a recognizable whole, Jennifer said, "Brad Hartley's taking Tracy's picture?"

Nora's stomach lurched. She hugged the pink calico cat pillow and said, "How do you know?"

"Know what?"

"That Brad's taking Tracy's picture."

"You just told me!"

"I didn't *tell* you," Nora said. "I *asked* you."

Jennifer took a deep breath. "How would *I* know? Why didn't you ask Brad?"

"I didn't think about it. I didn't think about anything! I mean, how can anybody think when Brad Hartley's smiling at her? So you don't think he's taking Tracy's picture?" Nora persisted.

Jennifer groaned. "Nora, could we please talk about something besides Tracy and her pictures?"

"I'm not talking about Tracy," Nora said. "I'm talking about Brad."

Unless Jennifer changed the subject, they'd be arguing in a minute. "Did you finish your homework?" she asked.

"I haven't even started," Nora responded. "I just got home." She remembered suddenly how annoyed she was with Jennifer. "I spent half an hour looking for you. Why didn't you wait?"

"I had to get home to do my homework. I've got a meeting tonight and — "

"You didn't have to run off like you did."

"I didn't *run* off."

"You didn't wait, either."

"I couldn't. You were so busy with Tracy — "

"There you go again," Nora said, "bringing up Tracy."

"Me? You're the one! Who went running off with Tracy at lunchtime and never came back to get me like she promised?"

"I was only trying to help," Nora defended. "Tracy is a very insecure person. She needs all the support she can get."

"Who doesn't?" Jennifer snapped.

A chuckle bubbled up inside Nora and escaped almost before she was aware of it.

It so surprised Jennifer that she giggled. "What are we laughing at?"

Nora's laugh exploded. "We're arguing!"

"We can't be! I made a special point of avoiding that." Jennifer caught her breath. "What are we arguing about?"

"That's what's so funny: I'm not sure."

"When you figure it out," Jen said, "let me know."

Chapter 7

Across the street from school, Tracy saw
the boys clustered at the foot of the front
entrance staircase. They were waiting for
her. She couldn't face another day of them
following her around, asking stupid questions, watching her every move. It was
unnerving. But how could she avoid them?
There were people at the side door, too. She
was directly across from the high school
entrance. She could duck in that way and
follow the connecting corridor through to
the junior high. Tommy Ryder often used
that route. He thought he was giving the
high school girls a thrill. Actually, if they
paid any attention at all, both the boys and
the girls thought he had a lot of nerve tres-
passing in their territory. What would
they think if Tracy paraded through their
halls? She'd have to chance it. Tommy and
Mitch were looking her way. If she didn't
do something quickly, they'd see her and

come running after her. Pulling her red scarf up around her face, she darted across the street and ducked into the high school.

Ahead of Nora and Jennifer, a girl, with her blonde hair flying, crossed the street and ducked into the high school.

"That looks like Tracy," Nora observed.

"What would she be doing going in the high school door?" Jennifer asked.

"You never know what Tracy's liable to do," Nora said.

"Oh, I don't know. She's pretty predictable if you ask me," Jen said.

"I don't understand you at all, Jen. I thought you liked Tracy."

"I do like her."

"Then why do you keep making . . . remarks about her?" Nora asked.

"Remarks? Me? I don't know what you're talking about, Nora. I'm the one who's always stuck up for her. You're always calling her a bubblehead or something."

"That was before. She's got a problem now, and you're certainly *not* interested in that."

"Just *what* problem are you referring to?" Jennifer's tone was cool.

"That's my point!" Nora countered. "You don't even know!"

Lucy fell into step beside them as they

turned up the walk to the junior high. "What's happening?" she asked.

"Ask her!" Jennifer and Nora snapped simultaneously.

Jennifer stormed off.

"What's with her?" Lucy asked Nora.

Nora shook her head. "I don't have the slightest. We can't even talk anymore without arguing." She mulled that over, finally coming up with a diagnosis: "It must be glands or something."

Mia huddled with Tommy and Mitch and a couple of other boys at the foot of the steps. At the edge of the group, Jason lounged against the railing. Halfway up the stairs, Susan and Amy chatted.

"Hey, Jen, have you seen Tracy?" Mia asked when Jennifer stormed past.

Jennifer gritted her teeth. "If one more person mentions that girl's name to me. . . !" Her voice trailed off as she stamped up the stairs.

Oblivious to Jennifer's fury, Mia called, "How about Andy? Have you seen him?" Then she shrugged and glanced questioningly at Jason.

"Don't look at me," Jason said. "I haven't seen anybody." He shifted his weight to his cast. "I don't get around like I used to. And without my skateboard. . . ." He shrugged. No one was listening. Just as well. He didn't really want to talk about it.

Apparently, neither did Mr. Donovan. Jason had waited an hour to see the man after school yesterday only to have the secretary tell him to come back another time. Maybe if he went inside now, he could catch Mr. Donovan before he got too busy. "Don't miss me too much," he said as he started up the stairs.

Tracy burrowed her head into her scarf as she threaded her way through the mass of high school students slam-banging their locker doors. The noise was earsplitting. Mr. Donovan was always telling the eighth-graders to turn down the volume. He'd never survive this! For Tracy, the commotion was welcome. No one noticed her. Feeling rather triumphant, she glanced back over her shoulder as she rounded the corner to the connecting corridor and bumped smack into Tony Hendrix. Her notebook slid to the floor and papers flew every which way.

Tony dived after them. "You still being chased?" he asked.

Tracy's cheeks flamed. "Yes. No," she said.

Tony laughed and handed her the sheaf of papers. "Which is it?"

Tracy's lower lip jutted out. She couldn't speak.

Mr. Donovan was busy with a parent.

Jason knew better than to wait around. Those conferences could go on forever. He went down the hall toward the cafeteria, concentrating on the rhythm his cast tapped on the worn tile. At the drink machine, he fished out some change and was just about to drop it in the slot when Tracy Douglas and Tony Hendrix entered the opposite side of the cafeteria and lingered there, talking. Jason shrank back against the side of the machine. He couldn't hear what they were saying, but he saw Tony put his hand on Tracy's shoulder and smile down at her before he turned and disappeared.

Denise appeared beside Nora. "Have you seen Tracy?"

"Not you, too!" Nora said. "Why is everyone looking for Tracy?"

"I don't know about anybody else, but I'm looking for her to give her a piece of my mind."

"She could certainly use it," Susan said. No one laughed.

"What did Tracy do?" Nora asked Denise.

"Drama Club was late getting out yesterday and I had to change and everything, so I asked Tracy to tell Tony I'd be right there. When I came out, they were both gone. I had to walk home."

"Did you ask Tony what happened?" Lucy asked.

Denise nodded. "He said Tracy was being bullied, so he took her home and then came back for me, but I wasn't here."

"Then why are you mad at Tracy?" Nora wanted to know.

"You don't think it was *Tony's* idea to take her home, do you?"

Nora's gaze slid upward toward Jennifer, who was standing alone at the top of the stairs near the door. "Did you ask Tony whose idea it was?"

"Of course I asked him."

"And he said it was Tracy's," Susan said, as though she had firsthand information.

"Actually he said Tracy pleaded with him to drop her off on the corner and go back for me, but, knowing Tracy — "

"She batted her baby blues at him," Susan anticipated.

"You don't believe your own brother?" Amy asked incredulously. Everyone knew how close Tony and Denise were. It was hard to believe Denise didn't trust him.

"I believe him," Denise said. "I mean I'm sure he *thinks* it was his idea. He probably didn't even realize what Tracy was doing."

Susan guffawed. "Most of the time, *Tracy* doesn't even realize what Tracy's doing."

Anger rose in Nora and splashed over. "I don't believe I'm hearing any of this! Tracy Douglas hasn't done anything!"

"Does she ever?" Susan asked.

Ignoring that, Nora continued, "Somebody starts pasting her pictures all over school without her permission, and as a result, she gets blamed for everything!" Her nose in the air, she brushed past her friends and stomped up to the school's double doors, where she said to Jennifer, "Did you hear that?"

"If it's about Tracy," Jennifer said, "I don't want to."

The bell rang.

Nora and Jennifer were both swept inside by the tide of rushing students. Down the hall near the bulletin board they were caught up in a logjam.

Nora jumped up to see over the heads in her way. "Jen, can you see what's going on?"

Jennifer craned her neck. "Looks like another picture of you-know-who. There's someone else in the picture, but I can't tell who it is."

"Jason?"

"I don't think so. It's a boy, though."

Nora had to know who was with Tracy in this latest picture. The crowd began to thin out and by the time she reached the front, Nora had an unobstructed view.

Still, she could not believe her eyes. There, for the whole world to see, was a picture of Tracy Douglas standing with BRAD HARTLEY!

Nora was suddenly aware of someone watching her. At the same time, she realized her mouth was open. She closed it and shifted her gaze to the left.

Andy Warwick leaned against the wall beside the bulletin board, dangling a key chain. He indicated the picture with a tilt of his head. "What d'ya think?" he asked Nora.

"I don't like it," Nora snarled. "It's a rotten picture."

Andy ran his hand over the tuft of yellow hair on the top of his head as he squinted at the picture. "You think so?" He stepped back and tilted his head to one side. "Looks good to me. Not as good as the one with Jason maybe, but not bad. Not bad at all. The thing is, you've got to keep things in proportion. That's the hardest part."

"Tell me about it," Nora said ironically.

Tracy shoved the remaining papers into her notebook — she'd have to sort them later — and headed for homeroom. If she timed it right, she could get there just as the second bell rang. That way, no one could bother her. Down the hall outside the office, a few of her classmates milled around near the bulletin board. Tracy slipped into the girls' room.

Nora was late for homeroom, and Mr. Mario made her go back to the office for an admit slip. That meant passing the bulletin board again. She just wouldn't look at the picture, she decided. Her resolve held until she came out of the office. Then she couldn't resist the pull of the photo drawing her eyes to it like a magnet.

Brad Hartley, she said silently, trying to make her mind believe what her eyes saw. Tracy must have tricked him into this. He wouldn't allow someone to take this picture voluntarily. Or would he? Maybe he had taken it himself! Only yesterday, she'd seen him with a camera. No one else was running around with one. She imagined him placing the camera on a tripod and peering through the viewfinder to set up the shot: *A little to the left, Tracy. Now a little to the right. That's it! Don't move! Beautiful, Tracy. Beautiful.* Then he'd activate the self-timer to delay the shutter until he could run around to stand beside her. And while the seconds ticked off, he might even have smiled at her!

At her elbow, Lucy said, "Doesn't that one look exactly like the others?"

"This one's unique!" Nora responded, turning to Lucy just as the girl stepped into the office with the attendance list. Lucy had commented the day before on the similarity of Tracy's expression in all the pictures, Nora remembered. Is that what she meant now? Nora stepped nearer the board for a closer look. But all she could see was Brad. Even though the picture was in black and white, she could see the blue of his eyes and feel them looking directly at her.

Jennifer came up beside her. "Nora, what are you doing? Mr. Mario sent me to get you. He said if you don't get back immediately, he'll give you a white slip."

Nora was so absorbed in the picture, she barely heard. "Jen, look at this picture!"

Jennifer glanced at the picture and shrugged. "No big deal."

"It is too a big deal, Jennifer. That's not just anybody up there; it's — !"

"I *see* who it is, Nora."

"But he's standing beside Tracy!"

"It's only a picture, Nora. It doesn't *mean* anything."

"It means plenty," Nora sputtered. "Tracy Douglas is a — a bubblehead — that's what it means!"

Chapter 8

Every time the locker room door opened Nora asked whoever came in, "Have you seen Tracy?"

"She's been late for every class," Amy said.

"Every time I see her, she's going into the girls' room," Denise added.

Susan tucked her white blouse into her shorts. "She's probably waiting till no one's around so she can plaster some more of her pictures up."

"Oh, Susan, don't be ridiculous." Lucy was exasperated. "She's not putting those pictures up. I mean, there was one in the boys' locker room." She leaned over to tie her Tretorns. "She's probably sick or something."

"That wouldn't surprise me," Nora said. "*Guilt* can make people sick."

Jennifer laughed incredulously. "Guilt? About what?"

Susan was quick to take up. " 'I don't believe any of this,' " she quoted, mimicking Nora's tone when she had defended Tracy earlier this morning. " 'Tracy Douglas hasn't done anything!' "

Nora blushed with embarrassment. She had changed her position on Tracy quickly, she realized, but not without cause. Surely the others understood. Someone would come to her defense. Her glance flitted from one to the other. They stared back. She shifted from one foot to the other. "Yeah, well," she said, just to say something. Then she brushed past Susan and walked into the gym.

The blast of Mrs. Scott's whistle brought the others in on her heels.

Tracy reached the locker room door just as Mia came out of study hall with a note to be delivered to the office.

"I've been looking for you," Mia said.

Tracy heard trouble in Mia's voice. She didn't need more of that! The whole morning had been a disaster. She'd been late for every class, and to top it off, her notebook was in such a mess, she'd handed her math assignment in to Mr. Robards, her American History teacher, and didn't realize the mistake until she'd gotten a white slip for not having her math. Mr. Robards returned the math to her after English, but

when she couldn't find her history homework, he gave her a white slip, too. One
more and she'd have a detention. Her shoulders drooped. "I'm late," she said.

Mia barred the door with an out-
stretched arm. "What's between you and
Andy?"

Tracy sighed wearily. This whole thing
was getting out of hand. "Don't tell me
there's a picture of me with *him*!"

"Not as far as I know," Mia said, suddenly wondering why there wasn't. "Picture or not," she said, "something's going
on. Andy's never around anymore and — "

"Maybe you're just looking in the wrong
places, Mia," Tracy said. "I see him all over
the place."

Mia took that as an admission of guilt.
"Aha!" she said.

"What's that supposed to mean?" Tracy
asked.

"You know what it means," Mia responded. "And I'm warning you, Tracy
Douglas. . . ."

Tracy fought back tears. "If you think
I'm interested in your boyfriend, Mia,
you're wrong. Andy Warwick?" She forced
a laugh. "That's laughable."

"Oh, yeah," Mia challenged. "And just
what's wrong with Andy Warwick?"

Tracy took several steps backward. She
couldn't win. No matter what she said, Mia

was determined to be mad at her. "Nothing's *wrong* with him," she said, attempting to avoid all-out war. "It's just that I — I already . . . have a boyfriend."

Mia's mouth dropped open, and her arm wilted to her side. "You what?"

Smiling triumphantly, Tracy pushed open the door and sailed inside.

"Who?" Mia called after her.

"That's for me to know, and you to find out." Tracy threw the carefully said words over her shoulder, but all Mia heard was the swack of the door as it closed in her face.

Fortunately, Mrs. Scott didn't notice Tracy come in late and take a place in the back of the line. Everyone else did. Denise darted her a tight-lipped glance. Tracy knew that was because Tony hadn't waited for Denise the day before. Well, that wasn't her fault. She smiled wanly. Denise looked away. Tracy locked into Nora's narrow-eyed glare. Was she upset because Tracy was late? What other reason could *she* have? Tracy smiled sheepishly and shrugged to indicate that her tardiness had been beyond her control. Nora frowned. Tracy looked away.

After class, Tracy was the first one back to the locker room. If she hurried, she'd be out of there before the boys took up their positions in the hall.

Jennifer was in a hurry, too. She had to phone the animal shelter. No matter how she figured it, she couldn't work there the next day and still have time to canvas her entire area for Save the Whales donations.

Tracy climbed into her hot-pink pants and scooped the matching shirt from the bench. She had just put her arm through and was pulling it over her head when Denise and Nora came up beside her, one one each side of the bench.

"Tracy Douglas!" they both said. "I want to talk to you!"

"That's good," Lucy said of their performance. "With a little more practice on timing you could start an act: Here they are, ladies and gentlemen, The Echo Twins!"

Susan laughed.

Jennifer wondered fleetingly why Denise wanted to talk to Tracy, but she didn't have time to wait around to find out. She gathered her things and left the room.

Ignoring them all, Nora focused on Denise. "What I have to say to Tracy is more important than what you have to say."

Tracy popped her head through her shirt and looked at Nora with wide, round eyes.

"Who says?" Denise demanded.

Tracy's head swiveled toward Denise.

Nora put her hand on her hips. "I say."

Tracy looked at Nora.

Denise put her hands on her hips. "Listen, Nora Ryan, you didn't have to walk home yesterday like I did."

Tracy's eyes rolled toward Denise.

Nora took two steps forward. "A picture of a boy *you* like isn't on the bulletin board in the front hall with Tracy!"

Tracy swallowed and her eyes got even wider. *Brad Hartley's picture!* Was it possible? She'd have to get a look at that.

Denise took two steps forward. "You don't have to look at it, you know."

Nora leaned across the bench. "Even if I don't, everybody else will!"

Denise leaned across the bench. "So what?"

Tracy eased onto the bench and reached for her books through the tunnel the girls' heads made above her. She peeked out into the hall. A few eighth-graders walked past, but Tommy and the other boys were nowhere to be seen.

Tracy left the locker room. At the juncture with the main hall, she looked toward the cafeteria. The boys lounged outside the door — probably waiting for her. A group of seventh-graders passed by, headed in the direction of the office. Tracy melted into the group. A couple of girls glanced at her suspiciously, but no one said anything. When they made the next turn,

Tracy proceeded straight down the hall to the bulletin board, slowing when she saw Jason Anthony, standing on one foot — the good one — outside the office.

"Hey, Tracy," he said, "watch this." He hopped on his cast, made sure of his balance, then did a kind of off-center spin on the hard rubber bottom extension.

"Don't do that, Jason," Tracy scolded. "You'll — "

Mrs. Peters appeared at the office door. "Mr. Donovan can't see you now, Jason. Come back after school."

Mumbling to himself, Jason clumped off.

Tracy turned her attention to the bulletin board. Sure enough, there was the picture: Brad Hartley and Tracy Douglas. She liked the sound of that better than the look of it; this picture was no better than the others. She wore that same stupid expression, and as in the previous shots, the background was too fuzzy to identify. Even worse, Brad didn't seem to . . . fit. Though they stood side by side, he seemed much smaller than she. Still, it *was* Brad. The only person she'd be happier to see up there beside her was Steve Crowley. On impulse, she stood on tiptoe and stretched. Try as she might, the tacks at the top of the picture were just out of her grasp.

"You're not taking that down?" a voice said at her elbow.

Andy Warwick.

Tracy eased off her toes. "It's my picture," she defended.

Andy twirled a key ring on his index finger. "Yeah, but whoever put it up there might've had a reason."

"What? To cause trouble? Because if that was his reason — "

"Trouble?" The key ring spun off his finger and slid across the floor, coming to rest against Tracy's loafer. The small rectangular object attached to the gold ring and chain looked familiar. Tracy bent to pick it up, but Andy dived after it. "What kind of trouble?"

Out of her side vision, Tracy saw Mia swooping down on them, her black cape flying. Tracy looked around for an escape. Her English teacher, Mr. Rochester, came out of the office.

"Oh, Mr. Rochester, can I see you for a minute?" Tracy called as she ran after him.

Mr. Rochester stopped and waited. "Sure, Tracy," he said. "If you want to walk along with me."

She said, "Perfect!" and fell into step beside him, darting glances over her shoulder.

Behind her, Mia planted her legs, in their red and purple horizontally striped tights, far apart on the worn tile. "I think

I deserve an explanation," she challenged Andy, who asked, "About what?"

Mr. Rochester cleared his throat. "Why did you want to see me, Tracy?"

Tracy blinked. She had forgotten all about the teacher at her side. "I was wondering," she said slowly, searching her mind for something sensible to say. She remembered the mix-up with her homework assignments. "Did I give you my history homework?"

He looked confused.

"In English, I mean."

He nodded. "I thought that's what you meant," he said.

"My notebook got all mixed up this morning when I bumped into Tony Hendrix over in the high school," she explained. "And I gave Mr. Robards the math and then Mr. Geiger gave me a white slip because I didn't have it and then when Mr. Robards gave it back I couldn't find the history so he gave me a white slip, too, and I thought maybe I gave you the history instead of English, which is probably in my notebook somewhere unless I left it — the paper, I mean, not the notebook — in gym because I was in kind of a hurry to get out of there, but if you don't give me a white slip I promise I'll find it and get it to you by the end of the day. "She paused to take a breath.

Mr. Rochester nodded solemnly. "You don't have your English homework, is that what you're telling me?"

"No, not exactly," Tracy said. "I mean I don't know whether I have it or not. It depends on whether or not I gave you the history."

"You didn't give me the history, Tracy. You didn't hand anything in this morning."

"I didn't?" Now she'd done it. White slip number three coming up. "Then I must still have it — the English, I mean — not the history; I don't know what happened to that. I'll get it to you before school's over, I promise."

A strange smile played across Mr. Rochester's face. "I'll be waiting," he said.

Tracy smiled. "Thanks, Mr. Rochester," she said. "You're terrific."

"Don't be too quick to sing my praises, Tracy," he said.

Tracy had no idea what he meant, but there was no time now to try to figure it out; Tommy and Mitch had spotted her and were coming toward her. She ducked into the girls' room and began thumbing frantically through her notebook.

Tracy looked up when Jennifer entered the girls' lounge. "You didn't see my English homework in the gym, did you, Jennifer?"

Jennifer was disappointed to find Tracy here. She was hoping the room would be empty. Between the squabbling that had gone on all morning and her to-do list, which kept repeating itself in her head, she needed a little peace and quiet. She took out her comb. "What English homework?"

"Today's. I dropped my notebook this morning when I — " She broke off. If she mentioned bumping into Tony, Jennifer'd be mad at her like everybody else was. "When I got to school and everything fell out, and now I can't find my English. I promised Mr. Rochester I'd turn it in before I go home tonight."

Jennifer ran the comb through her long dark hair. "Mr. Rochester didn't give an assignment last night, Tracy."

"He didn't? But he said — " She tried to remember exactly what he had said. Mostly, he had just smiled at her in a funny way.

"You must have misunderstood him," Jennifer said. "Or maybe he was teasing."

That was probably it. In the beginning of the year, when Mr. Rochester replaced Mrs. Rickerts, who had left to have a baby, the eighth-grade girls immediately developed a mad crush on him and dogged his every step, trying to get his attention. He'd been reserved and uncomfortable then, but now that they thought of him merely as their English teacher, he seemed to enjoy teasing them gently whenever the opportunity arose. Tracy had certainly given him an opportunity this morning. She began stuffing the papers back into her notebook. "Well, I wish he hadn't done that," she said. "I've had about all the teasing I can take."

Jennifer sighed. "You're taking all of this much too seriously, Tracy. If you'd just ignore it. . . ."

Tracy got to her feet. "I could ignore Susan, I guess, and even the boys. At least they aren't mad at me. But Mia and Nora —I don't know what to do about them." She focused on Jennifer's mirror image. "What do *you* think I should do, Jen?"

Jennifer glanced fleetingly at Tracy's reflection, then focused on her own face. She hoped Tracy wouldn't notice the impatience in her eyes. She prided herself on her sensitivity to other people's feelings, but she just couldn't handle this. It all seemed so trivial. "You're making too much of it, Tracy. There are so many more important things in the world to worry about." Though Jennifer tried to soften the edge in her voice, Tracy's lower lip jutted out.

"Not in my world," she said.

"Maybe that's your problem. You should . . . find some interests or something." Jennifer dropped her comb into her bag and turned to face her friend. Putting her hand on Tracy's shoulder, she said, "Come on, Tracy, let's go have lunch."

Tracy smiled wanly. "Thanks, but I think I'll just stay here. I'm not very hungry."

Approaching the cafeteria, Nora saw Brad near the door, his camera to his eye. She hesitated briefly. Should she say anything to him about the picture? About anything? Just exactly what was the accepted procedure when a boy you liked and who you thought liked you suddenly turned up in a photograph with another girl? she wondered. She'd never seen a situation like that discussed in *Seventeen*. She squared her shoulders and plowed forward. She wouldn't say anything — not even *hello*. She wouldn't want him to think she was throwing herself at him. If he wanted to talk to her, let him make the first move.

Brad was startled to see Nora pop into focus in his viewfinder. He lowered the camera and smiled shyly, ready to say, "Hi, Nora." Before he had the chance, she marched past him as though she hadn't even seen him. His first thought was the picture — she was angry about it. But then he remembered the day before; she'd walked right past him then, too. At the time, he'd thought it was a mistake — she just hadn't recognized him. Obviously, he was the one who'd been mistaken. She didn't want to talk to him.

Nora sank to her chair at the group's usual table in the cafeteria. "Guess what just happened!" she exclaimed.

"Someone forced you to buy the casserole," Amy said as she looked at Nora's tray.

Nora shook her head. "I just saw Brad!"

"You're not going to eat that, are you, Nora?" Lucy asked.

"The rice tastes like wet wool," Susan put in.

"The rice isn't all that bad," Amy countered. "It's the zucchinis — "

"Isn't it *zucchini*?" Lucy interrupted. "The plural, I mean."

"Never thought about it," Susan said.

"Who cares?" Amy said. "They taste like erasers."

"More like pencil shavings," Lucy observed.

"Will you guys listen?" Nora pleaded.

Jennifer dropped into the chair beside Nora. "Tracy's in bad shape." She bit into an apple. "You ought to apologize, Nora."

Her face glazed with a "Did you hear that?" expression, Nora looked from one girl to the next. "Apologize? Me? For what?"

96

"For being mad at her."

Mia appeared at Lucy's elbow. She leaned in confidentially, an intense expression on her face. "Did you know Tracy's got a boyfriend?"

Nora pushed her plate away. "Yeah," she said. "One I'd like to have."

Chapter 9

"Tracy's not in the girls' room," Mia said after school.

Tommy crossed his arms over his chest. "You were in there so long, she's probably not even in the building!"

"I had to fix my hair, Mia defended.

Tommy glared at the wet-look electric-blue and bright orange spiked hairdo. "You fixed it all right."

"Don't blame me for your lack of taste," Mia snapped.

Mitch sighed. "Are we still looking for Tracy or what?"

"I think we should have a plan," Tommy said.

Mitch beamed. "A game plan, right."

"Like what?" Mia asked.

Mitch shrugged. "I just follow 'em, I don't make them up."

"Maybe if we split up," Tommy suggested, "each of us at a different door.

Then, if she's still here, we'll catch her when she comes out."

"I'll take the back door," Mitch said. That way he could run laps around the athletic field while he waited.

"Nobody ever goes out that way," Mia reminded him.

Mitch thought about that.

"That's why Tracy might," Tommy said.

"Right," Mitch said.

"Okay, so Mitch'll take the back door, I'll take the front door, and you take the side, Mia."

"What about the high school?" Mia asked.

"Tracy'd never think of that," Tommy said. "I'm the only one who has the guts to go that way."

They started toward their posts.

"Wait a minute," Mitch said. "What if I see her? What do I do?"

"Let us know," Tommy said.

"How?"

Tommy looked at Mia. She shrugged.

"Whoever sees her first'll have to run tell the others," Tommy offered.

"And what'll Tracy do while we're doing that?" Mitch wanted to know.

"Get away," Mia said.

"Have you got a better idea, Mia?" Tommy challenged her.

When Mia couldn't come up with one,

they agreed to give it a try and each took off for his post.

Weaving her way through the crowd at the lockers, Mia kept an eye out for Andy. He saw her coming and ducked into the boys' room. Intent with purpose, Mia not only missed seeing him, she walked right past Tracy.

Behind Mia, Nora glanced up from her locker. "I can't be seeing what I'm seeing," she said to Jennifer.

Jennifer closed her locker door. Following Nora's gaze, she saw Tracy midway down the hall, talking to Brad Hartley.

"Would you believe she'd do that?"

Jennifer slipped into her ski jacket. "Do what?"

"Talk to him!"

"Since when's there a law against that?"

Nora slammed her locker door. "What do you suppose they're talking about?"

"Whatever it is, they don't look like they're enjoying it." Jennifer started down the hall.

Nora grabbed her arm. "We can't go that way, Jen. They'll see us!"

Jennifer turned. "The front way?"

Nodding decisively, Nora began in that direction, stopping abruptly at the end of the bank of lockers. "We can't go that way, either."

"Why not?"

"That stupid picture."

"So don't look."

"I can't help it."

Jennifer sighed. "Nora, I have to get home. I've got umpteen million envelopes to stuff for tomorrow."

Nora shifted from one foot to the other, trying to decide what to do.

Brad glanced up. He caught her eye. Nora turned away. Jennifer said, "I'm going, Nora," and marched down the hall toward Tracy and Brad.

Nora skipped along backward. "Wait, Jen," she pleaded. "Couldn't we go . . . to the library? There's this book I've been wanting to — " She hit something solid. She spun around. Tracy was in Brad's arms.

Nora's mouth dropped open, and her eyes widened. For several seconds no one moved. Finally, giving them a wide berth, she backed around Brad and Tracy, right into Andy Warwick.

She caught up with Jennifer outside. "Did you see that?" she said furiously. "He had his arms around her!"

"What else was he going to do?" Jennifer said.

"Nothing, I guess. I mean she probably just threw herself at him."

Jennifer laughed incredulously. "Nora, you pushed her into him."

Nora dismissed that as unimportant. "I really can't understand Tracy at all. After all I've done for her — "

"Name one thing," Jennifer challenged.

"Whose idea was it to dress her up like you, tell me that?"

"It didn't work, Nora. And Tracy didn't even want to do it."

"Do you think that made it any easier?"

Jason was in the hall outside the office. "Don't tell me you came to see Mr. Donovan," he said as Tracy approached.

Tracy shook her head. "Mrs. Peters. I have to change a detention." Mr. Morris had given her the third white slip when she turned up in biology one whole period late because she'd fallen asleep in the girls' lounge during lunch.

"She just went somewhere."

"Now what'll I do?" Tracy said. If she couldn't change the detention to some other day, she'd be late for her baby-sitting job.

Jason shifted uncomfortably. No one could look sadder than Tracy. "She said she'd be back in a minute."

"I guess I'll have to wait." She drifted across the hall toward the bulletin board.

"Do you know who took those pictures?" Jason asked. He no longer believed she had anything to do with them. Tracy just wasn't capable of it.

Tracy shook her head. "When I saw Brad with his camera, I thought maybe he had something to do with it," she said, "but he didn't do it. At least he said he didn't."

"It couldn't have been Brad; he just started taking pictures. These are all be-fores."

"*Befores?*"

"Before braces," Jason clarified.

Tracy beamed up at him. "You noticed my braces?"

The way she said it — as though he had done her some kind of favor — made Jason blush.

Mitch leaned against the building and tried to catch his breath. If he wanted to run long distance, he'd have to work on his stride. It was too choppy. Football did that.

"Heads up!" Marc Johnson called from the field.

A ball sailed over the fence toward Mitch. He reached out and caught it.

Marc curled his fingers around the fence links. Though he had transferred to Cedar Groves from California weeks ago, he still looked tanned. "Hey, hey," he said in his offhand manner. "Don't you ever miss?"

"Try not to," Mitch said modestly. He was good and he knew it. He had "the touch."

A group of boys joined Marc at the fence. "We're all going to shoot baskets at my house. Wanna come?" one of them asked Mitch.

Forgetting his reason for being there, Mitch readily agreed.

Mia sat on the steps outside the east door and studied her fingernails. The luminous silver stars — one at the center of each nail — had lost their luster, and the black polish surrounding them was chipped. She dug into her lunchbox-purse for polish. She came up with: a can of mousse, two sticks of body streaker — one iridescent, one plain — four tubes of liquid eyeliner, black lip gloss, navy-blue lip gloss, colorless lip gloss (she flipped that one toward the trash basket beside the stairs. It was supposed to turn a different color on each person's lips; it didn't change at all on hers), a can of mousse makeup, a batch of empty gum wrappers, an unwrapped SweeTart with lint stuck to it, several loose beads — white and black — and three bent safety pins from a bracelet she'd made, a leaky ballpoint, two chewed pencil stubs, and three empty nail polish bottles — one fire engine red, one navy, one black.

She threw everything back into the lunchbox, retied her black combat boots, adjusted her black cape, and flew off along the walk. If she didn't hurry to the store for more polish, she'd never have the time to do her nails before dinner.

Tracy was surprised at how easily Mrs. Peters agreed to change her detention date. She was so effusive in her gratitude that the woman finally said, "You understand that I am not excusing you from detention, Tracy, merely changing the date."

Tracy nodded enthusiastically. "Oh, yes, I understand. Thank you, Mrs. Peters."

Smiling, the woman lowered her eyes to the paperwork on her desk. "Run along now, or you'll be late for that baby-sitting job."

Saying, "Thank you! Thank you!" she turned on her heel and dashed out of the office.

"What'd she give you?" Jason asked. "The deed to the school?"

Tracy paused to look up and down the hall. There was no one around. She felt as though she had been relieved of a heavy burden. The day wasn't a complete loss after all. And she'd have the entire weekend to plan for Monday. Smiling radiantly, she turned to Jason. "You know, Jason," she said, "my mother has this saying: In the long run, things work out for the best."

"She say anything about the short run?" Jason asked, but Tracy was already halfway down the hall.

She sailed through the connecting hall into the high school, down the corridor, and out the door without a hitch. There she stopped to look back at the junior high front entrance. The sight of Tommy Ryder pacing there immobilized her just long enough for him to catch a glimpse of her. For several seconds, it didn't register. Then, he let out a war whoop and raced to the side door. No Mia. He dashed around to the back of the building. No Mitch. He zipped back to the high school entrance. No Tracy!

Chapter 10

"Tracy has this strange effect on all the boys," Nora told her sister Sally. "They tease her a lot, but at the same time you can just tell they like her. Personally, I've always thought she was kind of a bubble-head."

Sally leaned close to her dressing table mirror to apply her eyeliner. "Maybe that's the reason."

"You mean boys like girls who aren't too smart? That sounds like something Tracy'd say. She even told me to play dumb in shop when I started liking Brad." Nora paused, remembering how, no matter what she had done, Brad hadn't paid much attention to her until she had gotten their stalled car running on the Washington trip. She could still see the look of admiration in his eyes that day. What a contrast it was to the bewildered look she had seen there after school today.

"I'm not talking dumb or smart," Sally said. "I'm talking vulnerability."

Nora lowered herself to the edge of Sally's bed. "You mean like 'open to attack'?"

"I mean *open*, period." Sally ran the pencil across her eyebrows in short, quick dashes.

Nora nodded knowingly. "The innocence act."

"Tracy isn't acting, Nora, it's who she is. She's very . . . optimistic and trusting. She'd never intentionally hurt anybody. That brings out the protective instinct in a lot of people."

"What about Brad? She knows I like him and she still — "

Sally whirled to face her. "What? Talks to him?"

"There's that picture of the two of them," Nora said.

"Nora, you want to save yourself a lot of heartache?" Sally stood up and wrapped her burgundy Danskin skirt over her bodysuit. "Don't believe anything you hear and only half of what you see."

"Which half?" Nora asked seriously, but her sister's responding laugh was too contagious to resist.

"We'll never finish all these in time," Jennifer said as she stuffed an envelope with material on the plight of the whale.

Sitting opposite her at the kitchen table, Jeff Crawford, the Manns' housekeeper, in his canvas LIFE IS UNCERTAIN, EAT DESSERT FIRST apron, folded the handouts and smoothed each with a ruler. "Plenty of time," he assured her. "You don't start canvassing until tomorrow afternoon."

"But I have to be at the animal shelter at nine, and — "

"Animal shelter," Jeff repeated. "I knew I forgot something. Mr. Katz" — he chuckled — "perfect name for an animal shelter manager! 'Mr. Katz, have you any cats'?"

Impatient with his digression, Jennifer said, "What about Mr. Katz?"

"He called," Jeff chortled. "Said you should call him when you got home from school."

"Great," Jennifer said as she reached for the wall phone. "If he can't find anybody to relieve me tomorrow, I'll have to stay until noon."

Mr. Katz was out. Jennifer left a message.

As she hung up, Jeff said, "Sorry, no Katz today," and he exploded with laughter.

Jennifer frowned. Usually, she enjoyed Jeff's corny humor, but lately she'd been so busy it unnerved her. "Jeff," she said, "be serious."

The telephone rang. Jennifer picked it up, expecting to hear Mr. Katz's voice

"You sound . . . funny," Nora said. "Anything wrong?"

"I thought it was the animal shelter." Jennifer tucked the receiver between her shoulder and her ear to free her hands for envelope stuffing.

"Could you come over tonight, Jen?" Nora asked. "I really have to talk to you. I've been thinking about Tracy and Brad — Tracy mostly. I talked to Sally about her and — "

"I can't. Not tonight," Jennifer interrupted.

Nora was disappointed. "How about tomorrow?"

Jennifer sighed. "I have the animal shelter tomorrow and then — "

"You have to save whales," Nora said, remembering. "Sunday?"

"We have to count the money and all that. I don't know what time I'll be finished."

Nora said, "Oh."

After a pause, Jennifer said, "Listen, Nora, I have to go. I'm waiting for a call from the shelter and — "

"Right, Jen. I should've known better than to bother you with *my* problems.

You've got more important things to do."

"Nora!" Jennifer protested, but Nora had already hung up.

"What's that all about?" Jeff asked.

Jennifer sighed. "Nora's all upset over a stupid picture somebody put up on a bulletin board at school."

"Her picture?"

Jennifer shook her head. "Brad — that's the boy Nora likes — and Tracy Douglas. I keep telling her it doesn't mean anything." She reached for another batch of folded fliers. "Even if it did, there are more important things in the world."

"Maybe not to her," Jeff said.

Jennifer felt a twinge of guilt. She hadn't been sympathetic, she knew, but on the other hand, Nora hadn't been too understanding, either. Jennifer was busier than she'd ever been; yet Nora didn't even seem to notice or to care.

Eric, Jennifer's nine-year-old brother, flew in the back door. "Cookies ready?" he asked Jeff.

"Soon as I frost them," Jeff said.

"I need them *now*," Eric whined.

"Your Cub Sccount meeting isn't until seven," Jeff reminded him.

"But we're going right from Matt's — he asked me over for supper — and he's waiting for me *now*."

"Invite Matt in, Eric, and we'll frost

them *now*," Jeff said and got up from the table.

Jennifer looked at the stacks of unfolded sheets. With no one to help her, she'd never finish. "*Now* what am I going to do?" she said.

Jeff threw a glance over his shoulder. "You might try smiling," he said gently.

"Smile, you're on *Candid Camera*," Jessica Ryan teased when Nora stormed into the kitchen for a glass of cranberry juice.

Nora's face tightened. "Mom, Jennifer Mann gives me a pain," Nora said.

Her mother peered at her over her reading glasses. "What did she do?"

"Nothing! That's the whole point. She hasn't got *time* to *do* anything."

"I know the feeling," Mrs. Ryan said, turning her attention to the open briefcase on the table in front of her. A lawyer for Legal Aid, she often brought work home.

"A person can't even *talk* to her anymore." Nora downed her juice, put the glass in the sink, and left the room.

"Nora!" Mrs. Ryan called after her.

Nora popped her head through the doorway.

"*I'm* here if you want to talk."

"Maybe later," Nora said. "I haven't got time now."

She dashed upstairs to call Tracy. The

girl might be spacy, but she wasn't malicious. She was, as Sally had said, optimistic and trusting. She obviously didn't know who was taking the pictures or why. Certainly the picture of her and Jason was meaningless; perhaps the one of her and Brad was equally so. In any event, Tracy needed a friend right now. By being nice to her, Nora could not only fulfill Tracy's need but also her own: to find out just exactly what was going on.

Tracy wasn't home. Nora didn't leave a message.

She's with Brad! The thought blew into her head like a whirlwind, turning her previous reasoning upside-down. Tracy knew exactly what she was doing. She'd always thought Brad was handsome. Nora had seen her get all fluttery in his presence. Somehow, she had made him like her. They were probably out right now, smiling at one another over pizza at Luigi's, the place of her own date with him.

"How dare he take her to the same place he took me!" Nora said aloud.

Then, on impulse, she dialed his number.

"Hello," a male voice answered.

Was it Brad's? Her heart pounded so loudly in her ears she couldn't be sure.

She cleared her throat. "Is this the Hart — " Her voice cracked. " — ley residence?"

"Yep."

She said, "Oh, I'm — uh — sorry. I must have the wrong number," and hung up.

It was after eleven when Jennifer closed the door to her room. The job was finally finished, thanks to Jeff and her father and Eric, who had all helped.

Wearily, she undressed and put on her nightshirt. She folded her white chenille bedspread to the bottom of the bed and climbed under her pink comforter. Bed had never felt so good. She fluffed the pillows behind her and leaned back against them, fingering the gold locket she wore on a chain around her neck. Inside was a picture of her mother and father. Her mother had died when she and Eric were very young. Jennifer had been thinking about her a lot. Usually, she didn't consciously miss her. Lately, she did. It was probably because she felt so pressured with her projects and her friends' problems. Everyone seemed to expect her to take care of things. Sometimes, she just wanted to slow down, to have someone — her mother — take care of her. Still, she knew she was lucky. Her father and Eric and Jeff were special people. But they were male, and sometimes, they just didn't understand.

Her mind jumped to Nora and Tracy

and all the commotion about the pictures. It leaped to Tony and their friendship. It skipped to the next day's canvassing. It hopped from whales to stray dogs to Mr. Katz. It was like a slide projector gone haywire, snapping pictures on and off so fast none came into clear focus.

Yawning, she reached for the diary on her nightstand. Writing in it often helped organize her thoughts. She shook the pen out of the its spine, rested the book against her drawn-up knees, and opened the blue leather cover. She flipped to an empty page and wrote, *Dear Diary*. Then, filled with uncertainty, she paused. The page looked so long and so empty and so white. It had been so long since she'd made an entry it was as if this were the very first time. She had to write something to still the jumble of thoughts inside her head, or they would keep her awake all night. She closed her eyes to think. Slowly, her knees slid down under her covers. Her head fell to one side. The diary dropped to the floor with a thud. Fast asleep, Jennifer never heard it fall.

Nora's conflicting feelings about Tracy kept her tossing and turning all night. In the morning, she decided to go over to the Douglases'. The only way to settle this was to confront it.

When she turned the corner to the Douglases' house, she saw Tracy coming out her front door, carrying a duffel bag.

"Tracy!" she called.

Tracy waved and smiled. Then, remembering Nora was mad at her, she vaulted down her front stairs and hurried along the walk.

Nora ran to catch up. "Tracy," she said at the girl's side, "can we talk?"

Without breaking stride, Tracy turned her head to look at Nora. Her blue eyes were wary.

The word *open* popped into Nora's mind. Sally had used it to describe Tracy's charm. Certainly, the girl couldn't hide anything. Her feelings shone in her eyes. People always knew where they stood with her.

"I'm not mad anymore," Nora said, not knowing for sure if she really meant it.

Tracy brightened and slackened her pace. "Oh, Nora," she said. "I'm so glad. I hate it when you're mad at me."

Her quick acceptance made Nora uncomfortable. "Where're you going?" she asked to shift the emphasis.

"Baby-sitting," Tracy said. "Wanna come along?"

"Won't the people mind?"

Tracy shook her head. "And the kids would love it. Twins. A boy and a girl."

Nora agreed to tag along. She had nothing better to do.

Tracy beamed. "You'll love them. They're trouble, but they're fun, too."

Except when her charges were sick, and she could pretend she was the attending physician, Nora never thought of babysitting as fun, only as a means to an end: having a little extra money in her pocket.

Three-year-olds Jamie and Janie threw themselves at Tracy the minute she walked in the door, each demanding to be held. Tracy knelt down beside them, hugging them and laughing.

Their mother seemed harassed. "Am I glad you're here," she told Tracy and Nora. "They've completely demolished the family room already this morning. And I tried to set the table for company tonight, but it was impossible. They took things off as fast as I put them on."

Tracy looked at the twins. "Are you giving your mother a hard time?" she asked with mock sternness.

They grinned sheepishly.

Mrs. Morse put on her coat. "Tracy has magical powers," she told Nora. "She's the only one who can handle them." Adding, "Good luck," she kissed the twins and hurried out the door.

Tracy held up her duffel bag. "I wonder what's in here," she said.

The twins' eyes sparkled with anticipation.

"Let's open it in the family room." Tracy headed in that direction.

The twins followed along, giggling excitedly.

The room was a disaster area. Bits and pieces of "unbreakable" toys lay strewn on the floor and furniture, along with poker chips, newspapers, cookie crumbs, and a number of other items Nora couldn't identify.

Tracy stood in the doorway, shaking her head. "There's no more room here. I guess we can't open the bag today."

The twins' mouths and eyes rounded with disappointment.

"We could clean up," Tracy suggested. "Then we could find out what's in the bag."

The twins nodded, and they and Tracy set to work. Tracy made the job such fun that the twins enjoyed doing it. In no time, the room was in order.

Tracy had a natural gift for knowing the children's moods and warding off a tantrum or tears. Her bag was full of tricks: Nerf balls, clay, colorful wooden puzzles, fingerpaints, hand puppets.

"You're really good at this," Nora said admiringly.

Tracy shrugged. "I like it," she explained. "Anyway, these two are easy. Last night I took care of the Osbornes." She went on relating her experience with those children, but Nora's mind lingered over the words *last night*.

Tracy had been baby-sitting. She wasn't with Brad.

When Mrs. Morse returned home, Nora and Tracy decided to go to Temptations. Along the way, Nora was filled with praise for Tracy, who accepted it with a simple, modest "Thanks."

"I just wish I was as good with people my own age," Tracy said.

"Everybody likes you," Nora assured her.

"Susan doesn't."

"Oh, well, Susan. She doesn't like anybody. She doesn't even like herself!"

"That's probably the reason she doesn't like other people," Tracy said.

That insight coming from Tracy left Nora speechless.

Tracy didn't seem to notice. "Nora, that picture of me and Brad —"

"I know there's nothing to it, Tracy," Nora interrupted. Embarrassed by her earlier suspicions, she didn't want to talk about it.

"Brad's really upset," Tracy went on. "He thinks you don't like him anymore."

"He told you that?"

Tracy nodded. "I talked to him yesterday. He said you walk right past him without saying 'hi' or anything."

"I thought he was the one taking the pictures," Nora said.

They fell silent, each preoccupied with her own thoughts.

After a while, Tracy said, "If only I could think of something to do about those creepy boys."

"You'll figure something out," Nora told her. "After seeing how you handled the twins, I think Mrs. Morse is right: You do have magical powers."

Nora couldn't wait to talk to Jennifer. Her day with Tracy had filled her with insight. Tracy was far more interesting than Nora had ever imagined. She remembered Sally's advice about believing only half of what you saw. Now Nora knew that what one saw might be only half of what was really there.

Chapter 11

Monday, on the way to school, Jennifer was filled with her experience of soliciting for Save the Whales. "People would open the door," she said, "and I'd open my mouth. Then they'd slam the door. I started thinking I was invisible or something. I mean, they didn't even give me a chance to say who I was or what I wanted."

"I'm surprised you didn't finish early, then," Nora said. She had phoned Jennifer several times over the weekend but had never reached her.

"I probably would have except for the people who invited me in and wanted to talk. I was at one house for an hour!"

"Did they give you a big donation?"

"They gave me reasons why they couldn't give anything. And then there were the people who talked a lot about reading *Moby Dick* in high school. They didn't give anything, either."

"Did you make any money at all?" Nora asked.

"Twenty-five dollars and thirty-three cents."

"Total?"

"That's *my* total. Disgusting, isn't it? I don't know about the *total* total."

"I thought you were counting it yesterday."

"We were supposed to, but some people didn't finish. I know of two who didn't even start!"

"Where were you, then? I must have called a hundred times," Nora said.

"I hung around the library for a while, waiting for people. Finally, I went over to the Children's Home. I'm in charge of the puppet show again. I don't know what I'm going to do about that."

"Talk to Tracy," Nora said. "I'll bet she'd help."

Jennifer couldn't believe her ears. No matter where she and Nora started a conversation, it always came back to Tracy. She was getting sick of the sound of the girl's name. "Tracy who?"

"How many Tracys do we know?"

"I sure don't know any who could help put together a puppet show," Jennifer said.

"That's what you think." Nora could hardly contain her enthusiasm. She'd been waiting all weekend to tell Jennifer about the Tracy she was getting to know. "Tracy is incredible! I went baby-sitting with her Saturday and—"

"I thought you were mad at her," Jennifer interrupted, irritation in her voice.

As they turned up the walk in front of school, Nora said, "Who can stay mad at Tracy? I mean if you knew her, Jen, she's—"

"I know her better than you know her," Jennifer snapped.

Nora sensed Jennifer felt the way she herself had felt at the beginning of the year, when all Jennifer talked about was Denise. "Anyway," she said, backing off, "it was a lot of fun baby-sitting with her."

Before Jennifer had the chance to respond, Mitch Pauley stuck a camera in her face. "Say cheese," he directed.

Tommy rushed up beside him, a camera to his eye. "Out of the way, Pauley," he commanded. "This is my shot."

Jennifer said, "Get out of my face," and Nora added, "Creeps," but without their usual intensity. A scene on the stairs had caught their attention, and they moved up the walk as if they were in a trance.

Everywhere they looked, eighth-graders were snapping pictures. They pointed their cameras at the building, the bushes fronting it, windows, doors, their own feet—

some took pictures of others who were taking pictures of them.

"What's going on?" Nora asked Lucy.

"Wait till I get this shot," Lucy said, aiming her camera at the top of Jason's red head. "There!" She advanced the film. "That should be great. I'll call it *Wheat Field at Sunset.*"

Jason said, "They've all flipped." At his feet, one of the other boys was focusing on the cast on his leg.

Andy lounged against the railing, his arms folded across his chest, a bemused grin on his face.

Mia trudged up, her camera on a tripod over her shoulder. "Stand still, Andy," she directed. "I wanna get a close up of your left ear."

"Why is everybody doing this?" Jennifer asked.

"So many people've signed up for the camera club, Mr. Mario'll probably have to cut some," Lucy explained. "I decided to get some practice. Brad gave me the idea."

"It looks like he gave everybody the idea," Nora said.

"Not me." Andy twirled his key chain around his finger.

"Stand still," Mia commanded him. "Wait a minute," she said as she stepped around the tripod. "What is that?"

Andy held it out for her inspection.

She took it from him. "It looks like a camera." She turned to the others. "Doesn't this look like a camera?"

Everyone agreed the small black rectangle with the red face did resemble a camera. It even said HOT SHOT MINI CAMERA right on it.

"It is a camera," Andy said.

Mia narrowed her eyes skeptically. "It can't be. It's too small." She turned it over. After careful examination, she said, "Very funny, Warwick." She showed it to the girls. "It's a coin holder." Mia had opened the rounded ends of what looked like a film cartridge; inside each were several coins. She handed it back to Andy. "I knew it wasn't a camera," she said smugly. "You didn't even sign up for the club."

"Some people don't have a chance," he said sadly.

Someone called out, "There's Tracy!"

The boys, led by Tommy and Mitch, stampeded down the walk and surrounded her, cameras clicking.

At Tracy's side, Amy slipped through the group and dashed to the safety of the stairs. "Hanging around with her is getting dangerous," she said.

Suddenly, the boys lowered their cameras and stepped aside, making a wide aisle for Tracy, who, looking triumphant, strolled past them to the foot of the stairs.

Amazed, Nora asked, "What'd you do, Tracy?"

"Oh, nothing," she said as she ascended the stairs. "Just showed them" — she spread her left hand out in front her — "this."

Everyone gasped. There on her ring finger, the back wrapped with string to make it fit, was a *boy's* ring!

Questions flew at her from all directions. Tracy fielded them with ease, a self-satisfied grin on her face.

"When'd you get that?"

"Yesterday."

"Where'd you get it?"

"At my house."

"Whose is it?"

"Mine."

"Who gave it to you?"

"A boy."

"Somebody from our class?"

"No."

"Where's he go to school?"

"He's in high school."

"Cedar Groves High School?"

The bell rang.

Tracy waltzed up the stairs, leaving everyone open-mouthed behind her.

"Tracy, who is it?" Lucy called as she dashed after her.

At the top of the stairs, Tracy turned.

"That's for me to know and you to find out."

Amy called, "Wait, Tracy!"

"I know who it is," Jason said, but the girls were already clamoring after Tracy.

Jennifer hung back. "Who?" she asked Jason.

"Tony Baloney," he said.

Jennifer's breath escaped in an amazed chuckle. "Tony Hendrix?" she said. "Come on, Jason. That's . . . ridiculous."

Jason shrugged and started up the stairs.

Jennifer followed. "What makes you think it's Tony?"

"I saw them together."

"Where?"

"In the cafeteria."

"When?

"Last week one day."

"What were they doing?"

"Talking."

One part of Jennifer dismissed Jason's claim as meaningless; another part felt a pang of jealousy. It was for that part that she said, "There's no law against that."

Jason went through the door, saying, "Guess not. There's no law against smiling at a girl, either, or putting your hand on her shoulder."

Jennifer stopped short. "He did *that*?"

Jason had merged with the crowd and didn't hear her.

Jennifer bypassed her locker for homeroom. She had to talk to Denise. She'd know if there was anything between Tracy and Tony.

Nora met her at the door. "Did you see the picture?" she asked.

Thinking *Tony and Tracy*, Jennifer felt a flutter of panic. "What picture?"

"Susan's. It's on the bulletin board by the lockers. Is she mad!"

Jennifer sighed with relief. "Where's Denise?"

Nora shrugged. "All Tracy's pictures are gone. Even the one in the boys' locker room — Mitch checked. His picture is back up on that board and on the one in the front hall."

Jennifer peered into the hall. No Denise. Where could she be?

At her elbow, Nora chattered on. "Susan's picture is awful! Worse than any of Tracy's. She's got this . . . smirk on her face."

Jennifer wasn't listening. Her mind was on finding Denise. Maybe she was at her locker. "I'm going to my locker," she said. "Tell Mr. Mario — "

Approaching from the opposite direction, Mr. Mario said, "You have something to tell me, Jennifer?"

Jennifer looked up and blushed. "No, I
— uh —"

Mr. Mario brushed past her into the
classroom, where he glowered at the boys,
who were arguing over whose camera was
best. "In the old West," he said, "weapons
were checked at the door. I think we'll follow that policy here."

"We don't have any *weapons*," Mitch
protested.

"A stone is not a weapon until someone
uses it as one," Mr. Mario said. He pointed
to his desk. "Put them there."

Grumbling, the boys surrendered their
cameras.

When Denise didn't show up for homeroom, Jennifer decided she had to get a look
at Tracy's ring. From the brief glance
she'd had, she'd thought it was a class ring.
Only juniors and seniors had those. Tony
was a sophomore. But the boys had re-
doubled their following Tracy, and getting
anywhere near her was impossible.

"Did you get a good look at Tracy's
ring?" she asked Lucy before English.

"I tried to during homeroom," Lucy said,
"but she kept her hand over it the whole
time."

Jennifer took out her grammar work-
book. "We'll see it in gym."

"There is no gym today, Jen. Don't you remember? There's that assembly."

She had forgotten. The fire department was giving a program on fire prevention. Now she'd have to wait until lunch.

Mr. Rochester directed the class to open their books. He went up and down the rows as each student in turn read a sentence choosing the correct verb form.

Jennifer couldn't keep her mind on verbs. Her concentration was on proper nouns — two of them: *Tony* and *Tracy*. Before she knew it, the girl ahead of her was reading a sentence. Panicky, Jennifer scanned the page. She'd lost the place.

Mr. Rochester interrupted the recitation. "Trust your ear," he said. "If it sounds correct it usually is. You wouldn't say, 'The pliers is,' for example."

Jennifer found her place. She read the sentence silently. *Mathematics (is, are) easy for me.* She thought of last week's problem of the week, which she'd completely botched, and that day's quiz, which she knew she'd fail. The room was uncomfortably silent. She glanced up. Everyone was looking at her, waiting. She cleared her throat. "Mathematics. . . ." She hesitated.

"Choose the correct form of the verb," Mr. Rochester prompted.

Jennifer looked at the sentence again.

"Neither one's correct," she said. "Mathematics *isn't* easy for me."

The class roared.

Jennifer kept her eye on the cafeteria door, watching for Tracy. "Did Tracy tell you who gave her the ring?" she asked Lucy.

Lucy shook her head. "No, but everybody thinks it's Tony."

At the end of the table, Mia was adding an orange stripe down the middle of her black nail polish. "I *know* it's Tony," she said.

"How do you *know*?" Jennifer challenged.

"Because I saw them together."

"Where?"

"She got in his car and drove off with him. He even had his arm around her."

Jennifer's heart sank.

"Big deal," Nora said. "He drove her home because you were chasing her."

Mia made a face. "We were not *chasing* her."

"When was all this?" Jennifer asked.

"I don't know what you'd call it," Nora said to Mia.

"Why didn't somebody tell me?" Jennifer persisted.

"We were just . . . looking for her, that's all," Mia defended.

"Nora!" Jennifer said. "Why didn't you tell me?"

Nora looked confused. "Weren't you in the locker room last week when Denise was looking for Tracy?"

Jennifer had a vague recollection of being there when both Denise and Nora came storming in after Tracy. "I think so, but — "

"Well, that's why Denise was mad. Tony took Tracy home without waiting for her, and Denise thought Tracy had talked him into doing that."

"I don't remember that," Jennifer said.

"Tony said it was his idea, but — "

"Aha!" Mia said. "Didn't I tell you?"

Jennifer felt suddenly clammy. "*Tony's* idea?"

"I don't think you were there, Jen," Lucy said. "I think you left before the good stuff."

"Where's Denise?" Jennifer asked.

"Her name was on the absence list," Amy said. It was her week to collect the slips from each homeroom after roll call and deliver them to the office.

"She must be sick," Nora said.

Tracy entered and Tommy and Mitch and two or three other boys rushed to her side, snapping pictures. Ignoring them, Tracy pushed her tray along the rail, and taking only Jell-O, crossed to the girls' table. The boys returned to their own.

Jennifer watched her approach intently, trying to get a glimpse of her left hand. Tracy set down her tray and pulled out the chair across from Jennifer with her right hand.

"Is that all you're going to eat?" Nora asked Tracy as she sat down.

Jennifer leaned forward. Tracy's left hand was out of view.

"Everything else has green things in it," Tracy said as she picked up her spoon with her right hand and let her left drop into her lap.

Amy poked a fork at the remains of her lunch. "You mean like mold?"

Pretending to reach for something on the floor, Jennifer peered under the table.

Tracy's left hand fluttered up out of her lap. "Like spinach and lettuce and other . . . green things," she said, using the hand for emphasis.

Jennifer sat up, bumping her head on the edge of the table. "Ouch!" she exclaimed.

"Green vegetables are good for you, Tracy," Nora said.

Tracy's hand settled back in her lap. "But I can't eat them," she said.

Her weight on her forearms, Jennifer

raised herself out of her chair and tilted to her right against Nora, who gave her a poke and asked, "What are you doing, Jen?"

"I forgot my toothbrush," Tracy continued, "and I can't go around all day with green things stuck to my braces."

Jennifer couldn't stand it another minute. "Tracy," she blurted, "don't you ever use your left hand?"

"Fingers don't work," Tracy said seriously. "I have to use the special brush Dr. Scott gave me with the ridge in the middle that fits over the wires."

Jennifer looked at her blankly.

Nora giggled. "I think Jennifer means she wants to see your hand," she translated.

"Oh," Tracy said and held up her left hand. The ring was gone.

"What'd you do with the ring?" Jennifer asked.

Tracy patted the neck of her sweater. "Around my neck," she said. "It kept slipping and everybody was bothering me about it. I thought it'd make a difference — having the ring — but the boys are even worse today than they were last week."

"Who gave it to you?" Jennifer asked.

Tracy sighed. "That's for me to know and — "

"Was it Tony?" Jennifer persisted.

Tracy blushed. "Tony Hendrix?" she sputtered. "Of course not. What makes you think that?"

Before Jennifer had a chance to respond, Susan marched up.

"Would you tell that creep to get lost?" she said.

The girls looked around.

"What creep?" Nora asked.

"Andy Warwick," Susan hissed, glancing over her shoulder. Andy, who had followed her into the cafeteria, was sitting with the boys. "He's been following me all morning."

Mia guffawed. "That's what I call wishful thinking," she said.

Susan dropped into a chair. "That picture of me on the bulletin board has caused more trouble," she said.

Tracy's eyes widened. "Then why'd you put it up there, Susan?" she asked.

Chapter 12

Dear Diary, I haven't written because I've been so busy. I'm still busy, but I just had to talk to you. Tracy Douglas is wearing a boy's ring, and everyone thinks Tony Hendrix gave it to her. Jason and Mia even saw them together! Tracy keeps telling everyone it's not Tony, but nobody believes her. I don't know what I believe. Tony and I are good friends. I think he'd tell me if he liked Tracy — unless he really liked her and was afraid to hurt my feelings. He thought I was too young to be his girl friend — at least that's what he said. If he's going out with Tracy, then that couldn't be the reason. I couldn't ask Denise about it, because she's sick. I called her after school (Tony didn't answer — I don't know what I would've done if he had!), but she was sleeping. And Nora's being really weird. She's, like, Tracy's best friend! She and Tracy and Amy and Lucy went to Tempta-

tions after school. I didn't go. I was sup-
posed to go over to the library to finish
counting money for Save the Whales, but
I came home instead.

The telephone rang.

Jennifer got up from the desk and crossed to her nightstand, where she picked up her pink princess phone. "Hello."

"Boy, do you sound draggy," Nora said. "I hope you're not getting sick or anything."

"Just tired." Jennifer settled into her red bean bag chair. "How was Temptations?"

"Awesome! You should've come. We had a real celebration. Tracy deserved it. The way she put Susan down at lunch was incredible."

"Did she say who gave her the ring?" Jennifer asked.

"She won't tell," Nora said. "Maybe no one did."

"Whatd' you mean?"

"Remember what she said at lunch about thinking the ring would make a difference — that the boys would leave her alone?"

Jennifer couldn't remember a thing about that conversation. She'd been too busy trying to get a look at the ring.

"Well, maybe she made the whole thing up just to make everybody forget about the pictures and leave her alone."

"Tracy would never think of anything like that," Jennifer said.

"It's just the kind of thing she *would* think of," Nora countered. "It's like what she did with the Morse twins: distraction."

"So she's a good baby-sitter — that doesn't mean anything."

"She's really smart about lots of things," Nora defended.

"I like Tracy a lot," Jennifer said. "I've always thought she was kind of . . . harmless, but you've really gone overboard."

Nora decided to leave that one alone. "You know what Brad told her?" she said, using her own brand of distraction. "He told her he still likes me. He was afraid *I'd* stopped liking *him*. Can you believe that?"

"Like I said, the picture didn't mean anything," Jennifer reminded her. "I'm the one who should worry."

"You? Why?"

"Tony — everybody thinks that's who gave Tracy the ring."

"I'm telling you, Jen, Tony only took Tracy home because Mia and the boys — "

"How do you know for sure?" Jennifer interrupted.

"Tracy told me and Tony told Denise."

"Jason saw them another time," Jennifer said.

"Doing what?"

"Talking and . . . smiling."

Nora chortled. "There's no law against that, Jen."

As much as she wanted to believe there was nothing between Tracy and Tony, Jennifer couldn't seem to let go of the idea. "No, but — "

"Jen, I don't know what you're upset about. I had a reason: There was a *picture* of Brad and Tracy. Besides," Nora added, "there are more important things to worry about." Even as she said them, Nora realized she'd heard those words before — from Jennifer. "Listen, Jen, I didn't mean — "

"Did you do your French?" Jennifer interrupted. It was bad enough having her own words thrown back in her face without listening to Nora squirm.

"I studied the vocabulary," Nora responded, relieved to be off the hook, "but I didn't finish the translation."

They went over the translation together. Then, as always, they discussed what they would wear the next day.

When they'd hung up for the night, Jennifer went back to her diary. She read the last two sentences, then added, *The way I'm feeling, I couldn't save anything — not even myself.*

Next morning, when Jennifer wasn't waiting on the corner, Nora thought she'd

missed her. She hurried off alone, hoping
to catch Jennifer to set things straight.
The night before, she'd meant to tell her
what Sally had said about not believing
everything you hear. All that talk about
Tracy and Tony was only talk — nothing
to worry about. But somehow it had come
out all wrong.

Jennifer wasn't in front of school. No
one had seen her. Nora waited outside as
long as she could after the bell rang, then
she raced to homeroom.

She could hear the noise from room 332
halfway down the hall. The second bell
rang. The commotion grew louder as she
approached. Good. That meant Mr. Mario
hadn't arrived yet.

"Made it," she said aloud as she breezed
through the door.

Crowded around the bulletin board at
the front of the room, the class instantly
hushed and turned as one to stare at her.

Nora giggled uncomfortably. "What's
going on?"

Tommy and Mitch stuck cameras in her
face. "Say cheese," they said in unison.

Nora grabbed for the cameras. "Don't
you dare take my picture!" she commanded. "No one takes my picture unless I
say they can."

"Oh, really?" Tommy said. "Then you

must know all about this." He swept his arm toward the bulletin board.

There, bigger than life, was *her* picture! The worst picture of herself she'd ever seen! And, if that wasn't bad enough, she was standing beside *Tony Hendrix*! Dumbfounded, she stepped forward for a closer look.

Someone behind her said, "Hi, Jen."

Nora spun to face her friend, simultaneously doing a spread eagle against the picture. Smiling sheepishly, she said, "Hi, Jen. I waited for you on the corner."

Her eyes on the part of the picture visible over Nora's head, Jennifer stepped tentatively toward the board. "Overslept," she said.

Nora stood on tiptoe and stretched her arm over her head. "That's good," she said. "I thought maybe you were sick or something."

Mr. Mario came in. "Take your seats," he directed.

Everyone scattered except Nora and Jennifer, who stood stock-still as though they'd been frozen to their spots.

Mr. Mario folded his arms across his chest and waited silently.

"Sit down, Jen," Nora whispered.

"You first," Jennifer murmured.

Mr. Mario dropped his chin to look at

them over his glasses. "I'll count to three, then you can both go to your places at the same time. Is that agreeable?"

Jennifer said, "Yes, Mr. Mario," at the same time Nora said, "No, Mr. Mario."

Laughter rippled through the room.

Mr. Mario's mouth shrank. "Go to your seats NOW!" he boomed.

Jennifer backed toward her desk. Nora eased away from the board.

"What do we have here?" Mr. Mario said. "Another picture?"

Nora and Tony! Jennifer halted in her tracks. Her jaw dropped.

Mr. Mario leaned close to the board. "Not very flattering," he said.

"I didn't have anything to do with it," Nora whispered urgently to Jennifer.

Mr. Mario shot her a look. "It *is* your picture?"

"Yes, no. I mean I — uh — wasn't —" Nora sputtered.

"You mean you don't know who took it, is that it?" Mr. Mario offered.

"Right," Nora said, never taking her eyes off Jennifer's stunned face.

Mr. Mario sighed. "I'd certainly like to find out."

"So would I," Nora agreed.

Appraising the photography, Mr. Mario said, "Whoever it is needs help."

"That's for sure," Nora said.

Jennifer was out of the room before the sound of the first period bell had died away.

Nora flew after her, but the boys blocked her way. By the time she managed to escape, Jennifer was gone. Nora raced down the hall with Tommy and Mitch at her heels.

Tracy bobbed out of the girls' room. "Pssst, Nora! In here!" She saw the boys and ducked back in.

Nora kept moving. At the first turn, she stopped abruptly. Tommy plowed into her. She gave him a dirty look and backtracked to the girls' room. Popping her head inside, she called, "Jennifer?"

"Oh, Nora, am I glad to see you!" Tracy said. "I have to talk to you!"

Saying, "Not now. I have to find Jen," Nora took off for the lockers. No Jennifer. She ran back along the hall toward room 108.

Jennifer was already sitting at her desk, her American history book open before her. When Nora sat down across the aisle, Jennifer turned her back.

Nora ripped out a piece of notebook paper. *Jen, I don't know anything about the picture. Honest!* She purposely dropped her pencil on the floor. As she leaned over to get it, she put the note on Jennifer's desk. Jennifer ignored it. Nora snatched it back. She added URGENT across the front and underlined it three times. Then she yawned and stretched and dropped the note on Jennifer's desk. Jennifer ignored it. Nora reached over and poked her.

"Miss Ryan, is there something you need?" Mr. Robards asked.

Nora slid down in her seat and opened her history book.

Jennifer avoided Nora the rest of the morning. At lunchtime, Nora searched all over for her. She found Tracy in the girls' room.

"Jen been in here?" he asked.

Tracy shook her head. "Listen, Nora, I have to talk to — "

"I don't know what I'm going to do," Nora interrupted. "She's so mad at me."

"She's mad at me, too," Tracy said.

"She'll get over being mad at you, Tracy," Nora said. "You're not her best friend." Nora began pacing. "She only thought you were going with Tony because everyone else thought you were going with Tony, but now no one thinks that because they all think I'm going with Tony so that's what Jen thinks, too."

"Why did everybody switch?" Tracy asked.

"Because there's a picture of me and Tony on the bulletin board in our home-room."

"Oh, Nora," Tracy said sympathetically, "what are you going to do?"

"I don't have the slightest."

Tracy's face creased in thought. Suddenly, she brightened. "Here, wear this." She fished the ring out from inside her sweater and slipped the chain over her head.

"I can't wear that ring," Nora objected.

Tracy's expression clouded. "You're right. It won't work. It just made things worse for me."

"Whose is it?" Nora asked.

Tracy sighed. "My father's." Adding, "I had to do something so I made up the story about a boyfriend," she dropped the chain over her head.

"Tracy, you're really nutsy. What we have to do is find out who's taking those pictures; that's what we have to do!"

"That's what I wanted to talk to you about," Tracy said. "I think it's Andy Warwick."

Nora laughed incredulously. There was just no way it could be Andy Warwick. Photography wasn't his thing. He hadn't even signed up for the camera club. Like Mia, he was interested only in punk rock and outrageous clothes and hairstyles. "Right," she said sarcastically and started toward the door.

"No, wait, Nora. He has this . . . key

chain and it looks just like a camera
and — "

"It's a coin holder," Nora said.

"It sure looks like a camera to me."

"I saw it up close, Tracy. It's a coin
holder."

"Maybe he's got two," Tracy suggested.
"Because he's always . . . around lately.
Everywhere I go — there's Andy. It never
used to be that way."

That was true. Nora herself had bumped
into him more often than usual in the past
week or so. "But why would he go around
taking pictures of people and putting them
up all over?"

Tracy shrugged. "Andy never does
things the way normal people do."

"I can't worry about it now," Nora said
as she pushed through the door. "I have to
find Jen."

Tracy ran after her. "Where have you
looked?"

"Everywhere!"

"The cafeteria?" Tracy said.

"That's the only place I haven't looked."

Jennifer was at their usual table along
with Amy and Lucy.

As Nora and Tracy approached, Tommy
and Mitch fell into step behind them, making horns with their fingers behind the
girls' heads.

At the table, Nora said, "Jen, I've been looking all over for you. You have to listen."

Tommy pulled out a chair for her.

Nora gave him a dirty look and went around the table to take the chair beside Jennifer.

Jennifer turned her back.

"I don't know anything about that picture," Nora said as she dragged the chair around to Jennifer's other side.

Jennifer turned away.

"Let me get *your* chair, Tracy," Tommy offered.

Tracy didn't trust the gleam in his eye. He'd probably pull the chair out from under her as she sat down. She circled the table.

Mitch got there first. "She wants *me* to help her, Ryder," he said smugly.

"That's what you think, Pauley."

"That's what I know, Ryder."

While the boys argued, Tracy sat down beside Jennifer.

"Let me sit there, Tracy," Nora said. "You sit here."

Tracy and Nora made the trade. Jennifer swiveled toward Tracy. Nora stood up.

"Would everybody just sit someplace," Lucy said. "You're making me nervous."

Jason appeared beside Tracy. "What're we playing? Musical chairs?"

Nora sat down. "Jennifer," she said, "this is ridiculous."

"Jason!" Tracy exclaimed. "Your cast is gone!"

"Jen," Nora pleaded. "Will you please look at me!"

"How's your leg?" Tracy asked. "Can I see it?"

Jason pulled up his pants leg.

Amy shook her head. "Give me a break; I'm eating lunch here."

Tommy pulled up his pants leg.

Mitch pulled up his pants leg.

"Jennifer," Nora pleaded.

Lucy and Amy took their trays to the next table.

"Does it hurt or anything?" Tracy asked Jason. "It looks so . . . pale."

"And skinny!" Tommy said as he shook his pants leg down.

Mitch compared Jason's leg with his own. "It looks . . . dead!"

"Would you please listen at least," Nora said.

Jennifer stood up and silently left the table.

Smiling, Jason sat down beside Tracy. "Soon's I get my skateboard back, I'll be good as new."

"When'll that be?" Tracy asked.

Jason shrugged. "Eventually."

Tracy frowned sympathetically. "That's when the orthodontist says I'll get my braces off."

Nora dashed after Jennifer with Tommy and Mitch at her heels.

At the cafeteria door, Brad Hartley said, "Hi, Nora."

Nora didn't see him.

"You're the only one who noticed my cast was gone," Jason said.

Tracy smiled broadly. "And you're the only one who noticed my braces — of the boys I mean."

Jason zeroed in on Tracy's smile. Braces or not, it sure was an eye-catcher. "Some people don't see what's right in front of them," he said.

Chapter 13

After school, Nora and Tracy examined the picture on the bulletin board in room 332.

"It's just like the ones of me with Jason and Brad," Tracy said. "Tony doesn't fit."

Nora stepped close to the picture. Tracy was right. Although Tony was standing next to Nora, his image was considerably smaller, as if he had been farther from the camera. The word *proportion* flashed into Nora's head. *The thing is, you've got to keep things in proportion.* Where had she heard that?

"It's like all the pictures with two people are two pictures," Tracy said.

"That's it!" Nora exclaimed, giggling with the excitement of discovery. "Tracy, you're a genius!"

Tracy looked around as though she thought Nora might be talking to someone else. "Me?"

"This is two pictures spliced together to *look* like one."

Tracy beamed. "Like they do with movie stars to make people think they're dating when, sometimes, they don't even know one another?"

Nora nodded. "And all those pictures of you? Lucy kept saying they looked alike."

"They did," Tracy put in. "All the same dumb expression."

"They were all the same picture, Tracy, don't you see?"

Tracy wasn't sure. "You mean whoever took them took the same picture over and over?"

"He took *one* picture and then changed it — used just the head and shoulders for the first picture and all of you for the ones with Jason and Brad." Nora turned her attention to her picture with Tony. "Now, if we only know who took them."

"I still think it's Andy Warwick," Tracy said.

Nora hardly heard her. She was already planning her conversation with Jennifer. "I can't wait to tell Jen," she said.

"Do you think she'll believe you?"

"Of course she'll believe me. Why wouldn't she believe me?"

Tracy shrugged. "You didn't believe me about Brad."

Nora sobered. "She'll believe me. She has to."

Jennifer got into bed and propped her diary on her knees.

Dear Diary, she wrote. *Things are worse today than they were yesterday. There's a picture of Nora and Tony on the bulletin board in homeroom, where I have to look at it for thirty minutes every morning. And Nora's running around like Ms. Innocence. She and Tracy are thicker than ever, and I think I know why: As long as everybody thought Tony liked Tracy, Nora could go after Tony behind my back. Nora has probably been interested in him all along — even when she was telling me he was too old for me.*

The telephone rang. Eight o'clock. *Nora.*

Jennifer reached over, picked up the receiver, and hung it up without answering. She had nothing whatever to say to Nora Ryan.

Nora heard the click of the receiver. "Some friend you are, Jennifer Mann!" she snapped into the silence that followed. Then she slammed down her own phone.

She began to pace. If Jennifer'd only listen — or yell at her! Something! Anything! It took two to fight and two to make up. She couldn't do it alone. She grabbed her pink calico cat pillow from her bed and threw it across the room. "Maybe I won't even try," she said aloud. "Maybe I won't talk to her either. Ever!"

I will never, ever speak to Nora Ryan again!!!

Jennifer ended her diary entry with such force she broke her pencil point on the last exclamation point.

Sighing, she went to her desk for another pencil. The drawer was jammed. She slipped a ruler in and worked to release it. She got it open and took out her treasure box, the top of which had caused the problem. She looked inside. The miniature pewter whale Tony had bought her was on top. Underneath were several pins from her collection: THE CENTER OF LIFE IS IF, EXTINCT IS FOREVER, TODAY IS THE FIRST DAY OF THE REST OF YOUR LIFE. At the very bottom was a blue-green crayon stub. She lifted it out carefully and ran her fingers along its smooth surface. Nora had given it to her in kindergarten. Then, it was new — Nora's favorite color — given as a token of friendship. Before that, Jennifer had made her *N*s backward. With Nora's gift, she had learned to make them correctly.

* * *

The calico cat cushion looked sad standing on his head in the corner. Nora retrieved it and ran her hand along its outline. Jennifer had made the pillow for her birthday. It reminded her not only of all the birthdays they had shared but of other good times — and bad. It took both to make a friendship. She had to keep trying. You didn't abandon a friend just because she was infuriating sometimes.

She picked up the phone and dialed. It rang once. What if she doesn't believe me? Nora thought. Without proof, her theory about the pictures sounded hokey.

The phone rang. Jennifer was sure it was Nora again. She wanted to talk to her, but after the way she'd acted all day, she didn't know what to say.

The phone rang again.

Maybe I don't have to say anything, Jennifer thought. Just listen. She reached for the phone.

She'll never believe me, Nora thought. What I need is proof. She hung up.

"Nora?" Jennifer said into the silence. She waited, but no one responded. She couldn't blame her friend for hanging up; after all, she'd done it first. If only she'd answered on the first ring. . . . She sat looking at the crayon in her hand for a long time. Finally, she dialed Nora.

* * *

Nora dialed Tracy. If she was going to solve the mystery of the phantom photographer, she'd need help.

Nora's line was busy. If she's talking to Tony, Jennifer thought as she hung up, I'll never speak to her again! On impulse, she dialed the Hendrix number.

"Tracy, we have to find out who took the pictures," Nora said.

"How?" Tracy asked.

"For one thing, we'll go to the camera club meeting tomorrow."

"I didn't sign up."

"You don't have to *join*, just *go*."

"What good'll that do?"

Nora wasn't sure. Beyond the strong feeling that the pictures were somehow connected to the club, she hadn't thought it through. "Do you have a better suggestion?"

"We could ask Andy if he did it."

"Andy couldn't be the one, Trace; he isn't smart enough."

"I've never been able to tell *what* he is," Tracy said. "It's like he's hiding or something."

Nora laughed. With his outlandish hair styles and funky clothes, Andy was the most visible boy in the class. "Hiding? Andy? A person can't miss him."

"Yeah, but no one ever gets past the clothes."

Tracy's words jarred something in Nora. But she was too impatient just then to figure out what. She had to call Amy and Lucy. The more people in on this, the better.

"Is Denise there?" Jennifer asked.

"Jen? Hi," Tony answered. He was smiling; Jennifer could hear it in his voice.

"Hi, Tony," she said. Then she didn't say anything.

"Did you want to talk to her?"

"Who?"

"Denise."

"Oh, right," Jennifer said, feeling stupid. "Is she around?" That was even worse. Denise was sick. Where else would she be?

"I think she's sleeping, but I'll check."

"That's okay," Jennifer said. "I really wanted to talk to you." Quickly, before she could change her mind, she blurted, "Do you like Nora?"

After a pause, Tony said, "Nora. Is she that friend of yours who wants to be a doctor?"

Jennifer felt something loosen around her heart. The whole story — starting with

Tracy's pictures and the ring and ending with the picture of Nora and him —tumbled out.

"Jen," he said when she paused to catch her breath, "didn't you think I'd say something to you if I knew about any of this?"

"I didn't know what to think."

Tony laughed. "Next time, ask. I'll tell you."

The minute she and Tony ended their conversation, Jennifer dialed Nora. The line was busy.

Chapter 14

Nora hurried eagerly toward school. The more she thought about it, the more certain she was that her theory about the pictures was right. That day, together with Tracy and Lucy and Amy, she would unmask the villain and make up with Jen.

Jennifer saw Nora a block ahead. Running to catch up, she called, "Nora! Wait!"

Nora glanced over her shoulder.

Jennifer waved frantically. "Nora!" she called again.

No more silent treatment, Nora thought with relief. She took several halting steps toward her friend. As long as Jennifer was talking to her, she might listen, too. And believe her — even without proof. She began to run.

As the gap between them closed, each called, "I have something to tell you!"

They met, laughing.

"You tell me your news first," Nora

urged. "You didn't talk all day yesterday; you need practice."

Jennifer didn't argue. She was too excited to wait. "The pictures aren't for real — they're a trick!"

Nora's eyes widened with amazement. "That's what I wanted to tell *you!*" she said. "How'd you find out?"

"Tony."

"Tony knew?"

"He didn't know anything! That's why I know. But," Jen added, "that's all I know. I mean I don't know how the pictures were done or anything."

"You've come to the right person," Nora said in her newly discovered private investigator voice. "I have already solved the Mystery of the Phantom Photographer."

"Really?" Jennifer sounded awed. "Who is it?"

Nora laughed. "I don't know *who*, Jen — only how." As they walked the last block, Nora filled Jennifer in on her thoughts. She wanted to ask Jennifer to go to the camera club meeting, but knowing how busy her friend had been lately, she decided against it.

Across the street, Tracy called and waved.

As they waited for her to cross, Nora said, "Tracy thinks Andy's been taking the pictures."

Jennifer shot her an incredulous glance. "Andy Warwick?"

"Impossible, right?" Nora said, dismissing the idea.

Tracy fell into step with them as they turned up the school walk.

"Jennifer knows about the pictures," Nora told her.

Tracy beamed. "Then you're not mad at Nora anymore?"

"I wasn't exactly . . . mad," Jennifer said.

Nora laughed. "What were you . . . exactly?" she teased.

"How about me?" Tracy asked. "Are you still mad at me?"

Tracy's directness was one of the things Jennifer had always liked about her. At the same time, it was the one thing she disliked — at least when it was aimed at her. "No, I — uh " she sputtered uncomfortably.

"Because if you are," Tracy went on, "you shouldn't be. I made up the whole thing with the ring. But not Tony," she hastened to add. "I mean, I never once pretended that *he* gave it to me."

Jennifer laughed. "I'm not mad, Tracy. Really. It was stupid of me to be mad in the first place. I should've believed what *you* said and not listened to everybody else."

The air immediately outside school was

electric with excitement. Clusters of eighth-graders compared the pictures they'd been snapping all week. Others examined their cameras to be sure they were loaded for action.

Lucy and Amy came running down the walk.

"What's the plan?" Amy asked Nora. "You didn't say much on the phone except we should all go to the meeting."

"Did everybody sign up?" Lucy asked. "If your name's not on the list, Mr. Mario probably won't even let you in."

"We can do that when the bell rings," Nora said.

Jason came up beside them. "I'm getting my skateboard back after school," he said.

Tracy paused and smiled at Jason as the others moved on toward the stairs. "I bet you're happy," she said.

"Happy doesn't begin to describe it," Jason responded.

"Did Mr. Donovan give you any punishment or anything?"

"Nope. He practically begged me to come get it. He's been tripping over it all week." Jason squinted at Tracy. He cleared his throat. "Ah, Trace," he said, and shifted his glance to the sky. "How'd you like to come with me to the office after school to pick up the board? I could show you some maneuvers."

Tracy smiled broadly. Then, remembering her promise to attend the camera club meeting, she frowned. "Oh, Jason, I'd love to but — "

"Listen, Trace, that's okay," he interrupted.

"Look at that," Lucy said. "Tracy and Jason. Do you suppose those pictures . . . foretell the future or something?"

Nora and Jennifer exchanged expressions of horror. "I sure hope not!" they said simultaneously.

"So what's our plan, Nora?" Amy asked.

"Did anyone call Susan or Joan or anyone?" Nora asked. "Because the more people in on this the better."

"Susan's not coming to school today," Amy said.

"I wonder if she and Denise have the same thing," Jennifer said.

"No way," Amy said. "Susan's faking."

Nora nodded wisely. "A slight case of picturitis maybe?"

They all laughed.

"How are we going to catch the person who gave it to her?" Lucy asked.

"I don't have a plan exactly," Nora said. "I thought you guys might have some ideas."

No one was listening. Their attention was riveted on Andy Warwick, who ambled up the walk in a black tie and tails. An inch of white sports socks was visible between the hem of the black pants and the tops of his red and white Air Jordans.

Tommy Ryder let out a war whoop and vaulted down the stairs with his camera in hand.

"That's the most bizarre outfit Andy's ever worn," Lucy observed.

Mia heard her. "Isn't it awesome?" she said, and sailed past with her tripod over her shoulder to join Andy on the walk.

Tracy drifted to the foot of the stairs. "Andy shouldn't wear a tux to school," she said. "It's all . . . out of proportion."

"You mean *inappropriate*, Trace," Jennifer corrected her.

"It's both!" Lucy said, shaking her head over the suit's ill fit.

Something clicked inside Nora's head. " 'The thing is, you've got to keep things in proportion,' " she muttered. " 'That's the hardest part.' " It's was Andy who had said that to her about the picture of Tracy and Brad. At the time, she had thought he was talking about her reaction to the subjects of the picture. Now it occurred to her he might have meant something else entirely. Could Tracy be right? Was he the one?

Mr. Mario marched up the walk, pausing to give Andy the once-over.

Andy said, "Hi, Mr. Mario."

The man responded with his "What

next?" look and proceeded to the stairs.

Nora said, "I'll go in now and sign up."

"I'll go with you," Jennifer offered.

"You guys stay here and keep your eyes on everybody," Nora directed.

They trailed Mr. Mario inside, where he stopped at the bulletin board and took down the camera club sign-up list.

"Is it too late to sign up?" Nora asked.

He sighed and took a pen from his shirt pocket.

"Me, too." Jennifer said. She had a lot to do this afternoon, but attending the meeting was important. She'd been neglecting Nora and her other friends. Without care and attention, friends could become an endangered species, too.

Surprised and delighted, Nora smiled.

Returning her smile, Jennifer felt a part of things for the first time in a long while. "And Amy Williams and Tracy Douglas."

"Stop!" Mr. Mario said. "No more! Please!" He began ripping up the list.

"Does that mean we can't come to the meeting?" Nora asked.

"Of course you can come. Everybody can come. Everybody *is* coming. We'll meet in the auditorium. I just can't put your names on the list. There's no more room!" He dropped the pieces of paper into the wastebasket. "I'll have to divide things up," he said, more to himself than to the girls.

"Beginning, intermediate, advanced. Meet three different afternoons."

"The person who's been taking all the pictures — what group'll he be in?" Nora asked.

Mr. Mario thought about that. "His eye needs training," he said, "but he has a certain skill in the darkroom." He looked at the girls over his glasses. "Have you found out who our budding genius is?"

"Tracy thinks it's Andy Warwick," Nora said.

Mr. Mario sighed heavily. "That wouldn't surprise me in the least. Nothing that boy does would surprise me."

Back outside, Nora said, "Let's sum up what we know."

There was a long silence. Then Lucy said, "We know whoever's taking the pictures has a camera."

Jennifer looked around. "That includes two thirds of the class."

"But they've only been bringing cameras to school for a couple of days," Tracy piped up. "My pictures were taken before my braces."

Ignoring her, Amy said, "I don't think it's Tommy or Mitch. They'd want everybody to know if they did it."

"And it's definitely not Brad or Steve," Nora added.

Watching Mia struggle to adjust her

tripod legs for yet another shot of Andy, Amy said, "Has anybody thought it might be a girl?"

Lucy shook her head. "It isn't one of us, and if a girl from another crowd was hanging around all the time, we'd know. It has to be a boy."

Her eye on Andy, Tracy murmured, "It's a boy, all right."

Catching Tracy's eye, Andy raised the key chain as though he were taking her picture.

"Andy! Stop that!" Mia commanded.

"One with a very small camera," Tracy said.

"I've been thinking," Nora said. "Maybe it's Andy."

"Andy Warwick?!" Lucy and Amy said.

At the sound of his name, Andy looked at the girls and started forward.

"Stand still!" Mia ordered.

Tracy sighed. Everything pointed to Andy. Why wouldn't anyone believe it?

"I know it sounds farfetched," Nora said, "but he's been more interested in the pictures than any of the other boys. And Mia keeps complaining because he's been too busy to spend much time with her."

"And Mr. Mario said he wouldn't be surprised if Andy was the one," Jennifer said.

"And there's that camera," Nora added.

"Coin holder," Lucy corrected.

"Maybe it's both," Nora said. "Things aren't always what they seem."

"Neither are people," Tracy put in softly. She was watching Jason, who stood alone at the top of the stairs, hunched against the door. He looked so sad. She wished she could be with him after school. It'd be fun to see him come to life again with his skateboard underfoot. And he'd offered to show her how to use it. She'd much rather do that than go to some old camera club meeting. For what? To find out who was taking those pictures? She already knew.

"But why would he do it?" Jennifer asked.

Nora shrugged. "Who knows with Andy?"

"If we could figure out a way to get the key holder . . ." Jennifer mused.

"Or his backpack. Maybe he has something in there — pictures maybe," Amy suggested.

"Evidence!" Nora said. "That's a good idea."

Tracy walked purposefully toward Andy.

"How'll we do it?"

"One of us could distract him," Nora said.

"Which one?" Amy asked.

Tommy Ryder thrust a batch of pictures

under their noses. "Take a look," he said.

Amy brushed them away. "Can't you see we're busy here?"

"Creep!" Lucy added for emphasis.

Saying, "Your loss," Tommy retreated.

"Who wants to volunteer to keep Andy's attention?" Nora asked.

No one wanted the job. Each person stated her reason for refusing.

Finally, Nora said, "Tracy! She'd be perfect. She could get Andy's attention and — " She looked around. "Where is she?"

"Over there by Andy and Mia," Jennifer answered.

"You did *what*?!" Mia erupted. "Why didn't you tell me?" She stamped her foot and punched Andy in the arm.

Curious, the girls moved toward them.

"Let me see that!" Mia grabbed the key chain from Andy's hand.

"What's happening?" Nora asked Tracy.

"Mia's mad at Andy," Tracy responded.

Lucy laughed. "I never would've known it," she joked.

"Look at this!" Mia turned to the girls and held out her hand. "The coin holder snaps out and films snaps in. It's a camera!"

"I told you it was, Mia," Andy said. "I told everybody it was."

"But I didn't believe it," Mia said.
"Can I help that?"

Over their arguing, Tracy said, "He's been taking all the pictures."

"Why?" Jennifer asked.

"The camera club — he wanted to be in it."

"Why didn't he just sign up?" Nora asked.

"You know Andy. He likes to be different," Lucy said.

"He probably wanted to be discovered," Amy offered.

"That's exactly what he wanted," Tracy said. "He figured he had to do something big to show Mr. Mario he could do it, or Mr. Mario wouldn't let him join. He thinks Mr. Mario hates him."

Jennifer was overwhelmed. "Tracy, how'd you get him to tell you all this?"

"I asked."

Nora laughed. There they were making elaborate plans to trick him into confessing, and all the time he was waiting to be asked. "Tracy, you're a genius," she said.

Tracy looked around to be sure Nora wasn't talking to someone else. Then she smiled. "Thanks," she said and shifted her gaze toward Jason. "I'm not going to the camera club meeting," she said.

"You don't want to be Andy's talent scout?"

She glanced over her shoulder at Mia, who was still arguing with Andy. "Let Mia do it."

The bell rang. Everyone pushed inside.

Jennifer and Nora trailed along behind.

"There's sure a lot more to Tracy than I thought," Jennifer said, "and to Andy, too."

"Sometimes what we see is only half of what's really there," Nora said. At the top of the stairs, she asked, "You still want to go to the meeting?"

"Wouldn't miss it," Jennifer responded. "I can't wait to see Mr. Mario's face when he finds out it's Andy for sure."

Nora laughed. "I can't wait to see everybody's faces!"

They breezed through the doors into the front hall.

"I never thought a two-dimensional thing like a photograph could show so many sides of a person," Jennifer said.

Nora smiled broadly. "I get the picture," she said.

What happens when Tracy and Denise go for the same part in the class play? Read Junior High #8, STARRING THE EIGHTH GRADE.

Read All About
The Girls of Canby Hall!

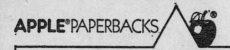